THE GREEN HERO

THE GREEN HERO
Early adventures of Finn McCool

by Bernard Evslin

illustrated by Barbara Bascove

Four Winds Press   New York

LIBRARY OF CONGRESS CATALOGING IN PUBLICATION DATA
Evslin, Bernard.
    The green hero.
    SUMMARY: Retells the early exploits of the legendary
Finn MacCool before he went on to become a great Irish
hero.
    1. Finn MacCool—Legends. [1. Finn MacCool. 2.
Folklore—Ireland] I. Bascove, Barbara, illus. II. Title.
PZ8.1.E957Gr   [398.2]   74–23851
                ISBN 0–590–07121–1

                Published by Four Winds Press
A Division of Scholastic Magazines, Inc., New York, N.Y.
        Copyright © 1975 by Bernard Evslin
                All Rights Reserved
        Printed in the United States of America
    Library of Congress Catalog Card Number: 74–23851
            1 2 3 4 5 79 78 77 76 75

For Dorothy
From Whose Eyes Green Takes Its Final Luster

Contents

Introduction

I followed Finn's trail right to his home grounds, and when I reached Ireland I hunted for him in libraries, bars, and country roads. In the libraries to read the ancient writings; in the bars to recover from the books and listen to the conversation; along miles and miles of misty country road to find the old storytellers who still spun their tales in occasional cottages, and who, I had been assured, could tell me stories never written. Every night I made a few notes about what I had seen and heard. Reading them over, I see that they may serve to set the stage for the entrance of that slender blue-eyed boy who did or did not live eighteen hundred years ago but who is more alive now than most.

Conversation in a bar near Trinity College Library, Dublin:
"Why Finn? Why not Cormac, or Cuchulain, Hound of Ulster? Or Conn of a Thousand Battles? Or Boru? What about McHuegal of the

Terrible Hand? Or the Fighting Sons of Usnach? Why Finn McCool?"

"Because he loses sometimes."

"What—Finn a loser? Is that what you're saying?"

"I think I'm saying he's the greatest hero of all. His world wasn't quite so simple. He loses and copes with his loss, and goes on to fight again. Also, he has to fight himself as well as the easier enemy. He's more interesting."

"Well, I guess that depends on what interests you."

"I guess it does. These other champions are too complete for my taste. Too invincible. They not only win every match, they take every round. It gets predictable. With Finn you never know."

"You're saying he's more human than our other heroes?"

"He's the only one remotely human. The others are muscleheads. They think with their swords. Finn has a live painful intelligence, ticking inside him. He wonders about things and puzzles them out. Cormac and Cuchulain and the others—they go to the battlefield in the morning and kill ten thousand before noon, and break for lunch, and kill ten thousand more before dinner. But Finn runs into trouble with every enemy. He has bad luck. And bad luck makes good stories."

"Mister, you don't understand the Irish. We've got to nourish ourselves on ideas of invincibility. How else could we lose every war we ever fought and still manage to consider ourselves the greatest fighters in the world—and make others believe it? Never mind your heavy-thinkin' in-and-outers. We need our all-conquering simpletons."

"Brilliantly expounded, sir. I buy it. And allow me to buy you another drink on the strength of it."

"Well, I'm not sayin' no."

"But let me put it to you. Which of your mythical heroes would have had the wit to say what you just said? Not the kingly Cormac, or Cuchulain, Hound of Ulster, or Conn of a Thousand Battles, or the baleful Boru, or McWhosis of the Terrible Hand. They expressed themselves exclusively in grunts and war cries. Only Finn had the magic gift of gab. In other words, he's not only more human than the others, he's more Irish. Or maybe that's the same thing?"

"Maybe it is, by god! Hey, Phil, there's a drought developin' over here. Bring this American connoisseur of Celtic wit another drink. Bring the Celt one too."

After a day at the Trinity Library: Spent the day, and part of the evening, buried in legends about Irish prehistory. A marvelous grab-bag. Each one begins at a different place. Some say the Fir Bolg came first, some say the Tuatha da Danaan. The one I prefer says the island was settled in time beyond memory by one race. But a monstrous tidal wave swept over the land and washed everyone out to sea. Those who didn't drown climbed ashore in Greece, and immediately began to carry leather bags of earth up the mountains to make vineyards. But after unknown time had passed, half of them still remembered the beautiful island of their ancestors because it kept appearing to them in dreams, and they turned their bags into leather boats and sailed back to Ireland. These were the Fir Bolg. Fir Bolg means leather bag. Years passed, or centuries. And those left in Greece grew restless too, felled trees, built ships, and sailed west. They called themselves Tuatha da Danaan, or People of Greece. Reaching an island, they found people who spoke the same language, and knew they had come home. They burned their boats so that the Fir Bolg would think they had arrived by magic, which the Fir Bolg believed. Finding that they were believed to possess supernatural powers, they began to use them. The men of the Tuatha da Danaan became wizards and the women were sorceresses. War poets sang magic runes that froze the enemy's blood and made the limbs of their own men swell with power. The women screamed at the mountain, turning heads to stones and stones to heads. The wizards hid rivers and raised forests. And a wizard physician of the Tuatha da Danaan filled a great well with crushed herbs into which he dipped the dead and wounded soldiers, who immediately revived and returned to battle. The Fir Bolg could not stand against this awful magic. They fled. The Tuatha da Danaan enslaved them and ruled Ireland.

After this victory the Tuatha da Danaan so dominated the imagination of the vanquished that they grew into gods. They lived in the green hills where they built wooden palaces of astounding beauty. In their orchards were trees that never failed. They feasted upon roast pig and good beer. And raided the lowland villages for mortal lovers.

Then, magically as they had come, they began to fade. They had lived too well and depended too greatly on magic tricks. Now real heroes were brawling on the plains, killing hugely, winning battles. And the pagan gods of Ireland, the Tuatha da Danaan, grew smaller and smaller in the popular imagination until they turned into elves and fairies. Those who had spoken in thunder and blasted hills with tongues of fire now could only sour milk and tie knots in the hair of dreaming girls. And as the pagan gods grew smaller, the pagan heroes grew larger and larger until they turned into giants.

Another legend of how things began:

Only the Irish know that Noah had four sons, not three as the Bible claims. This youngest son was a hellion and a wag. He mocked his father's weather forecasts and made unkind remarks about the huge clumsy boat the old man was building. Noah lost his temper and took after him with an axe, and the lad decided it might be wiser to leave home. But he must have learned something from his father, because when the flood began he was ready with a tiny ark of his own, upon which he stowed his young bride, two pigs, and two potatoes, and announced that he would sail far far to the west beyond people and beyond sin. He landed on an island now called Eire. His sons and daughters throve and multiplied—also the pigs and potatoes. But the waters never quite receded from that beautiful wet island, and have not to this day.

Why must we know about this last son of Noah? Because he became known as Cuhal ni Tyrne or King of the Wave in a tongue ancient beyond knowledge—and his descendants became the great clan Cuhal, of which Finn McCuhal was the last and greatest hero, and Finn's son, Ossian, the last poet.

Another day, another library. "File" (Fieleh) was the ancient name for poet. And this poet or storyteller—the terms were interchangeable—was prepared for his task by twelve years of precise and brutal training which broke ordinary men in a matter of hours. He had to learn a secret language as well as the transformation of ordinary speech; he learned magic, incantations, meter, composition. He memorized 350 tales—Destruction of Fortified Places, Cattle Raids, Courtships, Battles, Deaths, Feasts, Adventures in the Fairy World, Elopements, and Visions. After twelve years of this he was called File, and was empowered to tell tales of heroes, to wear a cloak of crimson and yellow feathers, and carry a golden rod. He ranked next to the king himself, and sat next to the king at table. Each year he received twenty-one cows and feed, food for himself and twenty attendants. He was allowed two dogs, six horses, and could grant safety from arrest for any crime except treason or murder.

The girls here have matchless complexions nurtured on fog and rain. I think of this as I gorge myself on the sight of the lovely long-legged young librarian who comes swinging through the brown light down the aisle, hugging an armful of tomes and offers them to me, smiling. She leaves me in no condition to appreciate *Colloquy with the Ancients, Annals of Tiglernach, Psalm of Cashal, The Speckled Book of McEgan, Book of the Dun Cow, Yellow Book of Lecan,* and *Cattle Raid of Cooley.*

I don't feel like reading, not at all. But she has brought me this heavy armful of books, and I owe it to her to use them. Besides, what else can I do? She's young enough to be my daughter, as if that mattered. But I sink myself in the books and pretty soon am more or less safely drowned. But I swim up again. I know her name, Nora McPhail; I saw it on a little plaque on her desk. McPhail . . . derived from MacFeile, perhaps, meaning child of the poet? Was she descended from one of those eloquent finely-honed bards who sat next to the king in their cloaks of crimson and yellow feathers? Shall I ask her the derivation of her name? With an opening like that I'd be able to present some fancy credentials. She's too pretty not to ask anything of. . . .

Very learned prefaces to these books. They discuss the unresolved question of whether or not the ancient Celts had a written language. They have found a kind of rock-writing composed of vertical and horizontal lines. Some say this was the ancient Celtic script called *ogham* . . . on the other hand it may have been birds sharpening their beaks. . . . The scholars dispute. What it seems to boil down to is this: The ancient Celts either had a written language and forgot it, or didn't have one and wrote in it anyway. . . .

The Celtic mythology does not abound in gods as do the other mythologies. But man was an uncertain quantity too. Gods and demons moved among men and within them. Heaven and earth intermingled. Nothing was as it seemed, and soon would be something else. Magic was the link. Everything speaks, everything lives in the ultimate fairyland. Why? Does the storyteller alone have the true perception? Scientists now have observed that there is motion in matter that was considered inanimate. Will they find voices in the abyss? Fabulists have always known that animals speak, the old stories are full of it. Men of science are questioning dolphins now to find out if this is so. Is imagination an uncanny form of insight? Some sinister sage once said that prophecy was memory of the future. Where did these stories begin, where do they end? Or do they? They flow beyond time, turn upon themselves, and flow back again. So it is fitting to end this beginning with Ossian, favorite son of Finn, who, in the manner of sons, came after his father—and was a poet of poets and told his father's story.

Ossian fought in Finn's last battle, and fell beside his father, but was not allowed to die. He was whisked away over the sea to the Land of Ever Youth, and dwelt there for three hundred years. Then, one day, fishermen casting their nets in the sea off Meath saw a giant gray stallion riding through the waves toward shore. On his back was a giant youth with blue-black hair down to his shoulders and eyes as blue as the core of flame. He was clad in antique armor.

"Finn," he called. And the trees bent under the musical blast of his voice. "Finn McCool! Where are you?"

He listened for an answer, then turned to the men. "What has happened?" he cried. "Why is everything so different? The land is overgrown with brambles and the men I see are small and weak. And there on that hill called Almhain where stood my father's castle all is waste and desolation. Where is he? Where is Finn McCool? I call him but he does not answer. And I do not hear his hunting horn from the eastern to the western sea."

The men told him that they had lived here all their lives, but remembered no castle on that hill. They had heard old tales of Finn McCool and the Fianna, but the warrior race had long passed from the earth, and they could tell him no more.

He turned to go, but saw a crowd of men, trying to lift a broad flat stone. They said:

"Come and help us, mighty hero, for you are a man of strength."

When he leaned down to move the stone, his saddle girths burst, and he rolled on the ground. Instantly the gray horse fell; its flesh withered, leaving huge white bones. And Ossian lay on the ground, a feeble old man.

The men lifted him and asked who he was.

"I am Ossian, son of Finn," he whispered, peering about with dim old eyes. "I fell with him in battle. I remember now. But I was not allowed to die. I was taken to the Land of Ever Youth where I have dwelt for these three hundred years."

"Have you come back to die?" asked a fisherman.

"I have come back to tell of my father, Finn McCool, and of the men of the Fianna, and their high deeds. For if the memory of Finn dies and falls to dust as has his mortal frame, then the honor of Ireland will die, and its men continue to dwindle until they shrink away to nothing. Give me a sip of water now, and hold me so I do not fall, and listen to what I have to tell."

The men did not wish to stay. The day was fading. The wind was sharpening. They wanted to draw in their nets and go home. But for all its feebleness the old man's voice held them. He fixed them with a glittering eye. They could not leave. He began to tell them what he had come to tell.

And here are the stories Ossian told, not as inscribed by dusty scholars and entombed in libraries, but in the sound of Ossian's own voice caught on the wind in the open air—that marvelous voice which was first heard as the dry cricket chirp of an old old man, changing slowly as the listeners gaped into a great freshet of colored sound full of laughter and excitement. For Ossian grew younger as he spoke. He pulled himself up and stood straight and tall until he stood there tall as a tree, full of strength and joy and the fiery sap of youth. He whistled in a certain way, and the bones of his stallion jigged together and put on flesh, and the tremendous gray horse arose from the dust, curvetting, neighing like thunder. Ossian leaped onto him and galloped away across the beach and disappeared into the mist. But before he left he promised to return and tell the adventures of his father after he became chief of the Fianna.

But that happens in another book.

Finn and
the Snakes

inn McCool was a giant but much too small for the work;
the runt of the litter he was, yards shorter than his brothers and sisters,
which was embarrassing. In fact, it is a better thing altogether to be a
large dwarf than a small giant. Such a thing has been known to spoil
a man's disposition entirely. But it didn't spoil Finn's. He quickly
learned how things were in the world, and said to himself:

"Can't afford to be bad-tempered, not till I get a reputation."

To go back a bit, though. When Finn was an infant he shared
his crib with a girl-baby named Murtha, whose own mother, a giant-
ess, had been killed by an avalanche she started herself by throwing
her husband headfirst off a mountain because he'd said something
rude. So Finn shared his crib with young Murtha, and his porridge
bowl, and his rattle, and such.

Now it is well known that infants are nasty squalling damp ob-
jects, except to their mothers, perhaps, but this Murtha was some-

thing else. Even as an infant she was beautiful. Her skin was ivory and pink, and she was never bald for an instant, but was born with a marvelous black fleece of hair, and had eyes that were neither green nor blue, but violet—rare for eyes. And teeth—a full set of them—so that she was able to bite Finn quite early. On the other hand, her smile flashed like a stream when the sun hits it. She was a lovely creature, and young Finn fell in love with her immediately, just like that, and had resolved to marry her before he was three days old, but decided to keep it secret awhile because he knew she wasn't ready to listen to proposals. Nevertheless, his love for her was so great that he couldn't rest for trying to win her admiration, which was difficult to do; she didn't seem to notice him particularly with her violet eyes, except when she decided to bite him or snatch his bottle. She would lie on her back dreamily watching the clouds go by—their cradle was a leather sling set in an oak tree; this is the way with giant babies—and he did not know what to do to attract her attention.

He noticed that she did not like slithery things. Worms made her unhappy. She would grab a wolfhound by his whiskers and kiss him on the nose, but spiders were a different matter entirely; she hated them and was afraid. This set Finn to thinking.

"My short time in the world has taught me that the way to a young lady's heart is by being very brave. Yes, even if you're not, you must make her believe you are; that's just as good. Now to be brave is dangerous sometimes, but if you're a lad of ideas you can get around that part maybe."

He thought and thought and put together a bit of a plan. "Now it's a fact she's afraid of worms," he said to himself. "This is quite plain. Oh yes, terrified of the tiny things, bless her heart. But why? They can't hurt her. They cannot bite or sting. Why then does she fear them? It is their shape, perhaps, for what else is there about them? And that they crawl on their bellies, squiggling along, for

what else is it they do? Now when a worm falls off the branch into
the cradle I might boldly brush it away from her, but that is not very
impressive, after all. She might appreciate it, to be sure, but she would
not go mad with admiration.* No, no. I must do something more
splendid, more bold, bigger altogether. What then is a big worm?
Big worm . . . why yes—a snake. That's anyone's idea of a big
worm, I should think. Now if she's afraid of worms, she would go
absolutely stark blue with terror, the beautiful child, if she saw a
snake, a sight she has been spared so far. If only I could rescue her
from a snake, ah that would be a thing to admire. This would count
as a great deed. This would win Murtha's heart. She would know her
cousin Finn is a hero, and fit to be wed. Yes, yes, I see it plain; I must
save her from a snake. There's a drawback though. I myself am by
no means partial to serpents. Why, as I lie here and think about them,
I can feel myself beginning to shiver and shake. I am still but a babe,
I haven't come into my strength, and I couldn't handle the loopy
beast if I did meet one. Nevertheless, for all the fear and doubt, there
is an idea here and I must make it grow."

So he thought and thought until his eyes grew blurred with
sleep, and the far stars trembled and went out. When he awoke, the
first tatters of morning mist were beginning to flush with light. He
swung himself out of his bullhide cradle, crept down the tree like a
squirrel, and went into the wood. As he went he kept his eyes open,
and kept thinking very hard. In the deep of the wood he rested himself under a tree. A strange bird screamed. Finn shivered. It was dark
in the wood, not the safe darkness of night, but a green scary dusk
of day half hidden. The bird screamed again. In the brush something
snarled and pounced; something else spoke in pain, chipmunk perhaps, or rabbit.

"All the things here eat each other," he said to himself. "The big ones eat the small ones. An uncomfortable kind of arrangement, especially if you're small."

He felt fuller of sadness than he could hold, and he wept a tear. The tear fell, but did not vanish as tears usually do. It glittered upon the leafmold, grew brighter, rose again toward his face. It was a tiny manikin, rising out of the earth. No bigger than a twig was he, with a squinched-up little nut of a face. Upon his head glistened Finn's tear, a crystal now, milky white as the moon, lighting up a space about the little man.

"Who are you?" said Finn.

"I am the Thrig of Tone."

"Are you now?"

"Have you heard of me?"

"No, sir."

"An ignorant lad you are then, for I am famous."

"What for?"

"Magic mostly. Mischief some. I'm much abused in certain quarters. But I'm a good one to know, I'll tell you that. Unless I happen to take a dislike to you, in which case you will regret our acquaintance."

"I see," said Finn.

"I doubt it. The thing about me is I'm not around very often, as it happens. A powerful curse is working upon me, you see. I'm the prisoner of a spell, woven by the wickedest old witch who was ever wooed by the devil and wore a black hat to her wedding—her name is Drabne of Dole. What can I do for you now?"

"You wish to do something for me?"

"I must."

"Why must you?"

"A condition of the curse. I'm a prisoner of the dust, you see, until the purest tear happens to fall on me. Then I come to life and wear it as a jewel and must serve the weeper, whoever it is."

"Did I weep a pure tear?"

"I'm here, am I not?"

"What makes a tear pure?"

"An extraordinary grief. Something outside the scheme of things, so odd it makes the gods laugh. And that laughter of the gods, which you know as the wind, means that someone somewhere has a grief he cannot handle. But it must be something special; plain things won't do, you know, not for the gods. They see enough of ordinary misery, they're no longer amused, they like something special. A crocodile moved to pity, perhaps; that roused me some time ago, and I had an adventure then. Or a king brought low. Yes, they like that. Or something wondrously beautiful made ugly, watching itself become so, and not able to stop. All this will set the night a-howling. What they found special in you, I don't know. But here I am. And there's the wind, hear it? What *is* your problem, lad?"

"Myself mostly. I come of a family of giants, and am small. I love someone who does not know what love is. And I have a bold deed in mind, but am afraid. Also, something pounced and something screamed, reminding me of the world's arrangements about big things eating small ones. Well, all this made me weep, Master Thrig of Tone, sir. If you help me I shall be grateful, but I don't know how you can."

"What is this deed you have in mind?"

"Well, you see, sir, this young lady I admire is much upset by the sight of a worm. Making me think that the sight of a snake would absolutely terrify her and make her feel very affectionate toward her rescuer."

"Think you'd be much good at fighting off serpents? They're very strong, you know, just one long muscle. Makes it awkward when you start to wrestle them. Not only that, but a mouthful of secret weapons. Hollow teeth that squirt poison, making even the smallest serpent deadlier than wolf or bear. You absolutely sure it's a snake you want to choose for your first bout, young Finn?"

"I am sure."

"Well, this requires a bit of thinking. Let's see. How can we do this with the most honor to you and the most effect on your little friend, and the least damage to both of you? And the most pleasure to the serpents, too, for they're the kind of creature that go along with nothing unless they're pleased. Pleased, yes, that's a thought. You play any musical instrument? Flute, for instance."

"Don't even know what it is. Sometimes, though, I shake my rattle a certain way that makes my blood dance. And Murtha sits there dancing without moving her legs."

"Rhythm section's all very well, but what snakes like is melody."

He broke off a reed from a nearby clump, took out a knife no longer than a thorn and notched the reed, then gave it to Finn.

"What's this?"

"A reed, doctored according to me lights."

"What's it for?"

"Well, reeds have a hard life. You must understand that in the vegetable kingdom they're nowhere. Very bottom of the list. No leaves, no scent, not even any nuisance value like weeds. They are frail stalks, bowing before every wind. And yet, this is their magic. Their courtesy to the wind is a very special quality. For they are the first to recognize this cruel laughter of the gods, and so are attuned to human misery. Their weakness gives strength its meaning; their lowliness makes fame shine; their pity is the best description in all the world of cruelty. The owl hitting the mouse, a wasp stinging a beetle to death, the young boy drowned in the pride of swimming, the bride realizing that she has married wrong and that her mistake has become her life—all these things that make the gods laugh and the winds howl, the reeds know first. They bow to it. And as the wind seethes through them, they rustle in a kind of music. It all becomes music in them. Music, which is the essence of all man cannot say in words. And, if you take a reed and notch it in a certain way—like this—and give it to one who will whisper his own story to it, why then a most exquisite music is made. And now happens the greatest joke of all, a joke on the gods themselves, those jesters. For hearing this music out of the reed, why Evil itself, the simplified shape of evil, the snake, becomes enraptured and dances in slow loops of ecstasy. And a slight pause comes to evil arrangements. Strength is diverted from cruelty. The blackness of death is split for a moment, and a crystal light streams, making pictures in the head, and it seems to those listening that things might be different, might be better. But only for a split second. Then the music stops and all goes back to the way it was before. But in that moment the snakes have danced and the victim forgotten fear. D'you follow me, boy?"

"Will you teach me to play this thing?"

"Let me hear you whistle a tune. I can do nothing if you have no ear."

Finn whistled. He could do that. He had amused himself in his cradle, imitating birds. The Thrig nodded.

"Not entirely tone-deaf, I'm glad to hear. Perhaps I can . . . maybe so. Very well, let us begin."

"Now?"

"Always now when it comes to learning, especially something difficult."

"But I'm hungry, I'm cold, I'm sleepy."

"Tell it to the reed."

Now it is said that the Thrig of Tone and young Finn stayed under that oak tree a week of days and a week of nights piping duets.

It rained sometimes, and the nights were cold. Nor did they stop for food. Nixies don't eat the stuff, and the Thrig had forgotten that humans do. All Finn had during this time was three mushrooms that happened to grow near where he was sitting. For his thirst he drank the rain. Oh, it was a difficult time he had, but it wasn't allowed to matter. The Thrig was a strict teacher, and kept Finn at it. What happened then was that the lad's hunger and thirst and sleepiness and loneliness wove themselves into the music, and the reeds added their own notes of pity and joy. And at the end of their time together under the oak tree you could not tell who was teacher and who was pupil; they played equally well.

They played so beautifully that the birds stopped their own singing to listen. Even the owl left off hunting, forgot her bloody hunger for a bit, and stood on a limb listening, hooting the tune softly to herself. The deer came, and wolves. Weasels, foxes, stoats, rabbits, bears, badgers, chipmunks, wild pigs. They came and stood in silent ranks at night, forgetting their enmity and fear as the moonlight sifted through the leaves and touched different fur with silver. Finally, two huge snakes came slithering out of their fearful nest and sat among their coils, weaving a slow dance.

"Enough!" cried the Thrig of Tone. "Lesson's over, young Finn. You've learned what I can teach. You can pipe and the devil can dance."

"Thank you, sir," said Finn.

"I have done my good deed without interruption, and am free at last, I hope, from the wicked enchantment which binds me to the dust and allows me to see the sun only once every thousand years."

"I hope so indeed," said Finn. "My thanks to you, O Thrig of Tone. Perhaps I can return the favor one day. Farewell."

And he went piping off through the woods, followed by various beasts.

But it's not so easy to get away with a good deed on this spin-

ning egg of a world. Evil has lidless eyes and does not sleep. At the
very moment that Finn was ending his lesson, Drabne of Dole, deep
in her hole, a thousand miles down, was gazing at a hand mirror,
combing her snaky hair with the backbone of a fish. Then the mirror
darkened; she could not see herself. And she knew that somewhere
on earth a good deed was being born. For good, the mere breath of it,
always darkened her mirror. She gnashed her teeth and stamped her
foot, crying:

> Oh grief, oh woe
> I'll not have it,
> No, no, no.
> Not a shred of kindness
> Not a ray of joy.
> I'll bend him, rend him,
> Tame him, maim him,
> Whatever he be,
> Large or wee,
> Man or boy.

So saying, she flapped her bat-wing sleeves and flew a thousand
miles in a wink of an eye to the old oak tree where the Thrig of Tone
stood gazing after Finn. She snatched him up and stuffed him into
her purse, and flew back a thousand miles to her den. She took him
to the stool where she sat to do her sewing, and bound him with
thread, and stabbed him with a needle.

> Stab and jab
> jab and stab.
> Better talk,
> better gab

"No," groaned the Thrig.

"Been doing good deeds again, haven't you? Let you out of my
sight for a minute every thousand years, and up you pop into the light
trying to help some poor fool do the right thing instead of taking life
as it is. Well, you'll tell me now what you did, and I'll undo it."

"Never," said the Thrig.

"Never's a long time, little one, especially when there's pain attached. You'll tell me, for I'll torment you till you do.

> I come and I go,
> I fly and I spy.
> I am Drabne of Dole
> I live in a hole,
> And I need to know.

"That's what witch means, small fool, Woman Who Knows. Now hear what I intend, Thrig of Tone, if you don't tell me straight. I'll round off your edges a bit and use you as a pincushion for the next thousand years. And it'll be pain, pain, pain all the time. I have plenty of tatters that need mending. My master's socks need doing too. His hooves, you know, they wear right through."

Thereupon she poked and prodded and jabbed and stabbed the poor little fellow until he could bear it no longer, and told her what he had done.

"Aha," she said. "It's a very good deed, indeed, but not too late to stop."

She threw him into her workbasket and stomped off to her big iron pot where it boiled over on its fire of brambles. She cast in the scale of a fishy thing that lives at the bottom of the sea and has neither sight nor touch nor any sense at all but is one blind suck. Henbane she added, and nightshade, wormwood, drearweed, and various poison fats that clog the sense, whispering all the while:

> In this cauldron
> stew and roast.
> Hearing ail,
> Music fail.
> Make him then
> Deaf as post.

A smoke arose from the witch's brew, curling in the spirals of a most evil spell, and wafted itself out of her den and up the long way into the world. Flew into the wood and fumed around the flat head of one of the serpents who were following Finn, drawn by his music. This serpent straightway fell deaf, heard nothing any more, but followed along anyway, no longer dancing, only crawling, filling with stupefied wrath.

Finn knew nothing. He went skipping and piping through the wood until he came to his own village, silent now, for it was the hot golden after-lunch hour when giants nap. He climbed into his bull-hide cradle and gazed upon young Murtha, sleeping sweetly as a folded flower.

"Sleep, little beauty," he said. "Sleep, my flower. Dream whatever dreams you do, and I shall sit here and my music shall steal through your ears and into your dreams, and when you awake you will hear the same music and not know whether you are awake or asleep, seeing me or dreaming still. And when the snakes come and frighten you, it will be with the slowness of nightmare, and in the darkened enchantment of that half dream you will hear me play and see me do, and watch the writhing evil dance to my tune. So you will know me for what I am, and love me forever. Sleep then, sleep until you awake."

He sat cross-legged and began to pipe again. The wolves came, and the deer. Bear, fox, badger, rabbit, weasel. They stood at the foot of the tree, listening. Then, sure enough, he saw the serpents unreeling themselves through the branches of the tree, winding down toward his cradle.

"Strange," he thought to himself, "they were mottled green, both of them, but now one has changed color. It's a dull gray, like lead. Oh, well, I suppose he has changed his skin. Snakes do, I hear. What's the difference? I'll play and they shall dance."

The green snake was already dancing, slowly winding fold upon mottled fold on the limb from which the cradle swung. But the gray snake had crawled into the cradle itself, filling it with great coils of dully glimmering metal hide.

Murtha was awake now, staring with stark-wide violet eyes at what had come into her sleep. And Finn thought that he was locked in nightmare. For this snake was not dancing. Its tiny eyes were poison-red and seemed to be spinning, making Finn's head whirl with fear. Not dancing, this serpent, but oozing toward Finn. He curled the tip of his tail around the lad's ribs and began to squeeze. Finn felt his bones cracking. He could do nothing else, so he kept playing. He sat there piping although the breath was being choked out of him. As his sight darkened he saw the snake above still dancing. And Finn, knowing that he was being killed, put all his pain and all his fear and all his loneliness into the pipe, and the pipe answered.

Now the green snake above danced on, filled with the wild sleepy magic of this music. The last exquisite strains of Finn's fluting plaited the snake's loops with slow joy, so that the coils he wove were made of living cable, stronger than steel. And when he heard the music growing dim and saw the gray serpent throttling Finn, he simply cast a loop about the strangler and pressed the life out of its body, all without ceasing his dance.

Finn felt the coils lose their deathly grip; his breath came free. In the huge joy of breathing he blew so loud a blast upon his reed that the giants awoke and came running to see.

What they saw was young Finn sitting in his bullhide cradle piping a tune, and a huge green serpent dancing, and another metal-colored snake hanging limp and dead, while violet-eyed little Murtha shook her shoulders and snapped her fingers and smiled like the sun upon water.

"Finn!" cried his mother, snatching him up and hugging him to her. "Are you all right? Has the murdering beast harmed you, child?"

"I'm fine, Mother. Put me back and let me play."

Finn's mother was not much for weeping, but she wept then.

"Don't cry, Mother. Take the silver one, and skin off his hide and make yourself a belt."

"I'll do that, son. And know it for the finest girdle in all the world."

The giants were whispering to each other. " 'Tis a wonder now. A proud mother she is this day. Young Finn's a hero for all his small bones."

"Save a bit of the hide to make a drum for Murtha here," said Finn. "Do that, Mother, and she will drum to my fluting, and all will be well."

"Do it I will," said his mother. "As soon as the beast can be peeled."

"Answer me, darlin'," said Finn to Murtha. "Will you have a silver drum and beat the measure as I play?"

The giants shouted their pride. The animals bayed and bellowed and trumpeted. A muffled shriek of pain came from Drabne of Dole, for witches suffer when wickedness fails. And the birds in the trees made a racket of glee.

Young Murtha though said nothing at all; she wasn't one for answering questions. Besides, she was doing something new. She stood among the snake's coils and danced along with him. He swayed, casting his green loops about her like a garland come to life. The giants then began to dance too, stomping the earth mightily, shaking the trees.

And Drabne of Dole, deep underground, whimpered and moaned and screamed, but no one heard her, for the day was full of joyful noise.

As for the Thrig of Tone, the witch's grief was his chance. He undid his bonds and escaped from her workbasket and made his way back to the wood. There he lives to this day, they say, doing sometimes good and sometimes mischief according to his mood, but mostly good nowadays for the balance is so much the other way. Children still get lost in that wood, and when they are found, say that a manikin with a face like a nut taught them to take music out of a reed. He wears a crown, they say, which is a single crystal, tear-shaped, full of moon-fire. Their parents laugh and tell them they were never lost at all but only asleep, dreaming. The children do not argue, but they know what they know. And it's a fact that children so lost and so found grow up fond of strange places and adventure. They go about the world confusing wind and laughter, tears and moon-crystals, teasing music out of reeds, heroes out of shadows, stories out of grief.

Finn Serves
the Salmon

The Crone-kin are not to be comfortably defied; they feed on foundered dreams and drink young tears like wine. So Drabne of Dole passed the word to her sister, the Fish-hag: "Finn's the one now. Catch him."

The Fish-hag was no idle witch, though. She had a job to do in the scheme of things. She guarded the Salmon of Knowledge to see that this important fish was not hooked by the wrong people or things learned by those meant to be ignorant. It was a hard job. Many there were who hunted the Salmon—Ireland has always been a land of scholars—and the Fish-hag had little time for tormenting a frisky boy. But Drabne was the elder of the sere sisters and had to be obeyed, so the Fish-hag set out baits for Finn.

She studied him awhile from hidden places and found that he belonged to that curious breed whose weaknesses do not matter because they are most surely betrayed by their gifts. Now Finn had many gifts, but they were still raw. An imagination that darkened the horses of the sun for night use, so that they galloped through his sleep, bearing him to certain hills and valleys where he knew he had been before. This was a gift, but raw. For he insisted on searching for these hills and valleys and green-lit meadows and echoing caves even when he was awake, and could not accept it when they were not to be found. Also, from the first he suffered from fear of being a coward, pushing himself to rash acts that were to pass for courage. And this trait of his was useful to the Hag, but she needed something else— and found it in his feeling for Murtha, which was his most advanced gift. For he was too young to be doing what he was doing, and that was attaching the idea of all grace and surprise to the image of one girl.

Upon a summer day then, Murtha, while wandering in a wood, heard a little voice speak her name.

"Murtha. Murtha."

"Who calls me?"

"Myself."

"Where are you?"

"Not where you're looking. Lift your eyes."

Murtha looked up. There, seated on a low limb of an alder tree, was an ugly gray bird with a pouchy beak.

"Good morning to you," said Murtha. "What sort of bird do you call yourself?"

"Pelican."

"Why is your beak made like that?"

"For carrying fish back to my nest."

"Are you a fishing bird then?"

"Am I not? The very best."

"What do you do so far from the sea? There are no fish here."

"I have come to see you, Murtha."

"Well, that's friendly of you. How is it you can talk at all, by the way? Is it common among pelicans?"

"Not very. But I'm a special bird, if I say so myself. I'm not only good at speaking but at guessing. I know, for instance, what you would like best in the world—an opal necklace with stones as big as hazelnuts, full of drowned lights."

"The very thing!" cried Murtha, clapping her hands. "I didn't know it was what I wanted most in the world, but now that you mention it I can't wait till I get one."

"And I'm here to tell you how," said the pelican, who was really the Fish-hag in disguise, of course. "A bit of way it is, past three meadows and a wood, up one hill and down two to a secret place. There stand nine hazels circling a spring. At the bottom of that spring is a bed of opals. Here must Finn McCool come in the first dawn, and if he questions me courteously, I will tell him how to dive for those opals, and you shall have a necklace finer far than any worn by any princess of any realm."

"I'll get them myself. I can swim and dive better than Finn."

"No, it must be he."

"Oh, pooh, why?"

"It is the way of things. The jewel a girl wears must be given her by a lad or it loses its luster. Now don't be wasting my time. Do you want those opals or not?"

"Oh, yes."

"Then go tell Finn what to do. Off with you!"

"Thank you, Mr. Pelican."

"*Miss,* dear. But you are welcome indeed."

The pelican rose heavily and flapped away. And Murtha, seeing the ragged wings and the stiff tail and the humped beak, felt her heart squeezed by a fear, for it seemed the shape of a witch riding a broomstick and not a bird at all. But then she saw the opals sliding

their lights about the slenderness of her neck, and she forgot her fear
and ran off to tell Finn.

Just as the windy sky showed its first apricot glow, Finn McCool
came to the place he had been told to go, past three meadows and a
wood, up one hill and down two. There he counted nine hazels hud-
dled in the mist about a spring of water. There was a curdling of the
mist as the boy watched, shivering with dread; it thickened into the
shape of a hag, who said:

"A fair morning to you, boy-dear."

"The like to you, mistress."

"And what brings you to the Spring of the Nine Hazels,
Finn?"

"I was instructed to come here."

"Indeed? And who did the instructing, may I ask?"

"Murtha of the Vale."

"Murtha, is it? How does she know of this place, and by what
right does she tell what she knows?"

"She was advised by a pelican to tell me to come here and fetch
her the opals that lie beneath the stream."

"Pelicans, opals, little girls who know more than what's good
for them and little boys who know less. This is a mixed-up tale you're
telling me, and I don't know that I like it at all."

The old woman wore a tattered cloak. She had wild feathery
gray hair and hands like the feet of a bird. Her nose bent to meet her
chin and the chin curved up to meet the nose halfway. Every time she
spoke both nose and chin moved, and Finn was so fascinated waiting
to see whether they would finally touch that he lost the drift of her
words.

"Why are you looking at me in that foolish way?"

"I am waiting to see whether your nose touches your chin. It comes closer each word. It's very interesting."

"Is it now?"

The Fish-hag smiled and Finn shuddered. Ugly as she was in the ordinary way, the look of her trying to be pleasant was not to be believed.

"Pray be not displeased, mistress. I meant no rudeness."

"Oh, you have a few lessons in courtesy to learn, but time enough, time enough. I have so much to teach you I don't know where to start."

"Are you a teacher?"

"Not by trade. But every good mistress instructs her own servants."

"I am no servant. I am Finn McCool."

"The very name I was given. Enough chatter, though. Lessons are bitter here, and the first of them is 'Shut up and listen.' "

He leaped away and started to run. She pointed her hands at him, muttering. A sewing basket floated in out of nowhere and perched between her hands. She continued muttering. A spool leaped out of the basket, rolled rapidly along the ground, hopping over twigs, and circled Finn, casting its thread about him, binding his legs. Though delicate as silk, the thread was strong as cable; he could not move. The spool rose in the air, still circling, and wrapped him about until he was cocooned from shoulder to foot. The witch whistled. The spool sailed back into the basket and paused to allow a needle to thread itself. The needle flashed out of the basket toward Finn. Darting more swiftly than a dragonfly, it sewed up his lips.

"The less you speak the more you hear. And for a learner, listening is a lot better than discussion," said the Fish-hag. "Any questions? No? Splendid. You've learned something already."

Finn felt his eyes fill with hot tears, but they were of rage, not grief. And when he thought the Hag would misread them, he grew angrier than ever, and the hot tears gushed.

"Yes, cry," said the Hag. "You'll learn it won't help, so you'll stop. Oh, I know it's painful, but pain is the beginning of education." She snapped her fingers. "Needle, thread, your work is done. Come back home, the lesson's begun."

The thread binding Finn was drawn back onto the humming spool in the Hag's basket, and the needle flashed back to its cushion. And now something truly fearful arose from the basket, a scissors flying like a bird snapping its steel beak. The scissors-bird darted in on Finn, nipped his ear till the blood came. Finn picked up a stick and batted at it, but the scissors-bird was far too quick and flashed in and out lightly, sticking and nipping the boy until he felt as though he had been rolled in nettles. He dropped the stick, and the scissors stopped biting, but sailed close to his head, snapping its jaws.

"He will be your tutor," said the Hag. "He is called the Scholar's Friend. He will keep you up to the mark."

So Finn became the Fish-hag's servant and learned certain duties about the pool. Simple ones at first. To feed small worms to larger ones, until the larger ones grew fat enough to be fed to the Salmon, whom Finn never saw plain, only as a silver flash when he rose at dusk to feed. He was taught to hunt plump tadpoles for the fish, and to peel them before casting them back into the pool.

"Truly, he's a delicate feeder, this fellow," said Finn to himself. "And I should not mind having a look at him at all."

For something had happened to Finn in his few weeks of servitude. He had grown used to pain and hard work and even to his fear of the circling scissors-bird and the hovering Hag. He had gotten used to his lips being sewn up tight. Since he could not speak with anyone else, he held long interesting conversations with himself. Indeed, tuned to listening as he was, and forced to take note of things as his painful lessons multiplied, he found himself growing more curious, needing to know how things worked, how they came to be, how they connected with other things. His biggest pain was the sense of being compelled to act in a certain way without his own wishes being consulted. He could not bear the idea of being considered a servant. But he found that concocting silent plans of vengeance, vividly pictured, enacted in great detail before sleep, helped him forget that pain, too. So he lulled himself each night with charades of violence done to the Hag, to the faithful denizens of her workbasket, to the Salmon, which he still knew only as a silver flash at dusk.

But then upon a day he was instructed to change the Salmon's diet. Preparations were under way for the great night of the year, the night of the Midsummer Moon, when the Druids were to assemble from near and far to eat of the Salmon, whose flesh would be magically renewed, and, having eaten, to return to their places with a belly full of wisdom to last the year. So worms and tadpoles were stricken from the menu. Now all that the Salmon fed upon was the hazelnuts shaken from the nine hazels. To Finn's surprise he was not instructed to crack the nuts, only to shake the trees so that the hard little bolls fell into the stream. He wondered about this.

And the Fish-hag who sometimes, disquietingly, seemed to be able to read his thoughts, said, "In these nuts lie kernels of wisdom. When such are to be swallowed, why then the jaws of the eater must be strong enough to crack the shells for himself."

Finn stole a nut and tried to crack it between his teeth. It was like chewing a pebble; all he did was give himself a toothache.

"Seems there's no shortcuts to these matters," said he to himself. "Well, I must look sharp then—to steal myself a taste of the

Salmon when the Druids feast. For, sure, I must learn enough at least to get myself free of this place and leave my mark on those who have done me harm."

Now by this time the scissors-bird had snipped the thread binding Finn's lips; it was understood that he had lost the habit of idle speech, and had learned to listen. Indeed there was little time for anything but preparation for the Druid feast. Three times each day he had to shake the nine hazels so that they would spill their nuts upon the stream, and the Salmon now struck the surface often to feed, not only at dusk. Finn admired the long lithe thrust of him. Smoothly armored in silver he was; like living coals dusted with ash were the eyes set in their flat sockets. When he opened his mouth it was full of glittering knives. All gullet he seemed, and the Fish-hag chanted:

"Look sharp, look sharp. Nothing is as hungry as wisdom, for everything must feed it, even hunger. So shake the tree, lad, shake it hard."

That night Finn could not sleep. He left the little kennel where he slept behind the Fish-hag's cottage and drifted over the meadow through the grove of trees circling the pool. The scissors-bird flew sentry as he wandered, not bothering to drive him back to his hutch, just keeping watch lest he try to escape. Finn sat on the bank staring at the pool. It was black as a tarpit. Then he saw a gliding sliver of light, and he did not know whether the moon was throwing darts from a chink in the clouds or whether it was the Salmon rising.

"It must be the moon," he thought. "The Salmon lies far below, fast asleep."

He heard a voice say: "Good evening, Finn."

"Good evening, sir."

"Are you sad, lad?"

"I cannot sleep."

"Then you are too happy or too sad. And I do not believe you are happy."

"True for you, Master Salmon."

"You're not old enough to be sad, Finn."

"What age do you have to be?"

"Old enough to have seen enough and done enough to have earned the right. What you think is sadness are silly little vapors of discontent, because you are not man enough yet to do what you have to do."

"And what is that?"

"Why, to free yourself, of course. To destroy your enemies and help your friends."

"You make it sound simple. I don't know where to begin."

"At the beginning, lad. Where else?"

"And what is that?"

"Name your enemies."

"Oh, that's easy. The Fish-hag, and her helpers—especially the scissors-bird."

"Very well, they'll do for a start. Destroy them, and your immediate troubles will be over, and you'll be ready for the next batch."

"But how? The Fish-hag is very powerful. She has magic on her side—flying needles, spools of thread that tie you up before you know what's happening, and that terrible scissors so swift and sharp, who can cut a lad to pieces as if he were a bolt of cloth."

"I'm sorry, Finn," said the Salmon. "I seldom give advice. And when I do, it's along general lines. No details. But seeing as you are rather young and tender, and may do some interesting things if you are permitted to live, I will stretch a point and tell you this. When faced by a powerful enemy, son, use their own weapons against them. Use their strength to your advantage. Seek your allies in the very heart of their camp."

"I'm sure that's good policy, sir," said Finn. "But I still don't know how to go about it. Dole me out a bit of your magic widsom, pray. Just one detail or two of real practical instruction."

"Why, for that, Finn, I would need more than your need. The only way you can learn such of me is not by questioning, but by eating of my flesh, the way the Druids do."

"But I am not a Druid, and if I steal from them I will be punished most horribly, the Hag has said. She will put me to the Fire Flick and the Marrow Log."

"Yes. Secrets and penalties, risks and rewards all go together, Finn. Farewell."

He flipped in the air and dived, and the water closed blackly over him.

"Well, some of it sounded like good advice," said Finn to himself. "If I can just figure out how to use it."

And he went back to his hutch and went to sleep. But the next morning he wasn't so sure. It's tricky being advised by moonlight; he did not know whether he had actually been conversing with the wise Salmon or if it had all been a dream. Suppose it had? Wisdom was sometimes offered in dream scenes; the old stories were full of it. Besides, he was never quite certain of how much he saw in his sleep and how much elsewhere.

But something had changed in him all the same. He found himself doing the first thing that came into his head, and that was a peculiar thing. Druids were gathering in the grove. They were clad in green—long beautiful leaf-green robes from which their clean gnarled faces shone. And Finn could see how they had come to be known as Tree Priests, Sages of the Mistletoe. When they doffed their green robes for a ceremonial wetting in the pool, Finn crept among the scattered garments, swiftly ripping each one. When the Druids emerged, dripping, and began to dress, there was a great outcry.

Their beards shook with rage; they scolded like great jays, grew hoarse as crows, cursing. And Finn was pleased to see the Fish-hag turn into their servant, scurry among them trying to appease them, vowing she would sew up every rip so that they would never know it was mended.

She squatted right there on the bank of the pool with her work-basket on her lap, and began to mend, needle swiftly flashing in and out of the green cloth swaddled about her. The scissors-bird swooped away from its perch near Finn and dived into the workbasket to be ready when the hag needed to snip. Now Finn had his enemy and her helpers busy doing something else. He left the pool and ran beyond the hazel copse to the Hag's cottage. It was the Sacred Salmon Net he was after, and he had to move fast.

The eyes of the Fish-hag's cat cast the only light in the room, but Finn lit no candle; he wanted it dark for his deed. Well he knew what dreadful punishments lay in store for him if he should be caught —just thinking of the Fire Flick and the Marrow Log was enough to scare a lad into obedience, and right then and there he almost abandoned his plan. But then the voice of the Hag creaked in his ears saying, "Do this," "Do that," and he thrust aside his fears and whistled the cat to him. The big black tom leaped to his shoulder; Finn felt its purr boiling beneath his hand as he twisted the cat's head now this way, now that, so he could see by the light of its blazing green eyes. The cat loved Finn, who, in his deepest trouble, found time to tease him with a dangled string and to toss him a peeled tadpole now and then.

Now the Sacred Salmon Net had come down from the earliest mists of time when the magic kings of the Tuatha da Danaan reigned in Ireland. Fashioned by Giobniu the great smith, it was spun of the beard of Mamos, the first Druid, and its handle was a rod of gold. When Finn snatched it off the shelf it seemed no implement at all

but a living extension of his own arm, and he knew he could scoop up any swimming thing from any water in the world.

Swiftly Finn left the cottage, bearing the net. Swiftly he circled the meadow where the Druids were matching verse while the Hag was mending, then darted through the hazel copse to the edge of the pool. And then, instead of dipping the net, stood there panting, watching the stars float upside down.

Finn stood at the edge of the pool; it seemed like a gulf of shadow waiting to swallow him. He stood there at the edge of wisdom, between boyhood and manhood, and was taken by a creeping blood-sucking sadness in which Murtha's face hung, now laughing, now cruel, garlanded by memory. And he stood there trying to fight the sadness and let the laughter and cruelty enter himself. He felt himself fill with a choking excitement. Now? he asked the night. Now! said the Salmon Net. Now! sighed the trees. Now! sang the drowning stars, and Finn dipped his net.

He needed but one dip. The net had barely grazed the water when the Salmon flashed out, curved in the air, and landed in the mesh. Finn felt the net come alive with the sudden weight of the great fish. It twitched out of his hands. He bellowed with rage and smote his head.

"Easy, Finn. Don't go breaking your skull like that—with so many others ready to do it for you."

Finn looked about for the voice and saw the Salmon standing on the shore wearing the net like a cape.

"Enough gawking, lad. You've caught me, now eat me."

"How shall I cook you, sir?"

"No time for cooking."

"What do you mean?"

"Eat me raw. Knowledge doesn't have to be palatable; it just has to be swallowed. And if you cannot stomach the truth, unflavored, why then you're not meant to be wise."

"But I am," said Finn.

Then, at the edge of the pool in the weird pearly fire of the midsummer moon, Finn ate the Salmon raw from nose to tail—flesh, bone, scales, guts, eyes—he ate every bit, and a terrible griping slimy meal it was. No sooner had he swallowed the last of it than he jumped into the pool, clothes and all, to wash himself clean. When he climbed back onto the bank there stood the Salmon, taller than Finn, looking like a prince in his close-fitting armor of silver.

"Now, Finn," he said, "I will tell you what you need to know."

"How do I escape the Hag?"

"Your first problem is this: having been eaten once, I am no longer available for the Druid feast, and our bearded friends are getting hungrier and hungrier. Listen, you can hear them railing at the Fish-hag."

Finn listened, and heard an angry chattering.

"I hear them. Where is the Hag?"

"At the cottage searching for the Salmon Net and not finding it. It won't take her long to figure out who stole it."

"What shall I do, wise sir, what shall I do?"

"Dip the net again. Catch the Loutish Trout."

"But the Druids have been eating salmon flesh for nine hundred years. Surely they know the difference between salmon and trout?"

"Not if you follow this recipe. Baste the trout in vinegar and butter, parsley, scallions. Dust it with wheat crumbs and crumbled madragore. Then lay strips of bacon upon it and broil it until the skin is charred. Stuff it with sautéed crabmeat, and serve with a sauce of almonds seethed in cream and sprinkled with poppy. Can you remember that?"

"Yes, sir."

"Do it, and so delicious will it be that the Druids will forget all distinction between salmon and trout, loutishness and wisdom, for they will be too busy cramming their gullet with both hands. Then, with bellies full and the drowsy fumes of madragore and poppy working, they will fall into a sleep so heavy nothing will wake them before breakfast."

"What of the Hag?"

"Oh, she will partake of the feast too, and will grow drowsy enough for you to strike a blow—that is, if you have followed my recipe, selected each ingredient, and done your baking and broiling for the proper time."

"What of the scissors-bird?"

"You'll have to handle him on your own. But quickly now, lad, or you'll flub the whole matter. Get cracking with that net and catch the Loutish Trout."

So saying, he dived into the pool.

"Wait," cried Finn. "I have questions to ask."

"No time left. I'll give you an all-purpose answer. To break a curse, make a verse."

And he disappeared.

Again Finn dipped his net and again it snared a fish—quite a different one this time, a fat trout with a speckled belly and a foolish face.

Finn cooked the trout as instructed, following the Salmon's recipe exactly. And exactly then did events befall as the wise fish had foretold. The Druids fell upon the savory dish and devoured it with gusto, smacking their lips and licking their fingers; and no sooner had each finished his portion than he stretched upon the grass in the deepest sleep he had ever slept, and the glade filled with the great snuffling drone of their snores.

The Hag had eaten heavily of the trout too, but when she felt

herself slipping into sleep, she knew that Finn had been taught to
trick her. Summoning all her uncanny will she propped herself
against a tree and with her last strength began to mutter into her
workbasket. Finn, seeing her do this, knew that he would soon be attacked by a swarm of needles and pins, not to mention the terrible
scissors-bird. He could not outrace them, he could not hide from them,
he could not ward off their agonizing stings. Then the last words of
the Salmon came to him. To break a curse, make a verse. And just as
the shining swarm began to rise from the basket, he shouted:

> Needle and pin
> So bright and thin
> And sharp as sin
> Put a stitch
> in Mistress Witch
> Sew nose to chin
> And chin to tree.
> Heed young Finn
> He'll set you free.

And, not believing his own power, he watched in ballooning joy
as the needles and pins turned in mid-air and flashed toward the warty
face of the Fish-hag. Swerving in bright patterns, the pins basted her
chin to the tree, and the needles sped after, trailing thread, and made
it permanent. But then something sliced through Finn's joy; it was
the scissors-bird clacking viciously out of the basket, and, try as he
might, Finn could not find a verse to turn this terror. He did not have
to. The one verse was enough. For the faithful scissors-bird snapped
about his mistress trying to cut the threads that bound her to the tree.
As fast as he cut them, the needles sewed them up again.

As his enemies were thus occupied, Finn strode away from the
pool, through the hazel copse, and across the glade where he had suffered much and learned more. Nor did he walk alone; winners seldom

do. The witch's cat leaped upon his shoulder and perched there like a heavy shadow grinning wickedly at the squirrels, and greening his eyes at troubled birds.

It was this huge black tom that Finn tried to give Murtha as a gift.

"Keep your cat," she said. "It was opals you promised, and opals I must have."

"I'll keep looking," said Finn.

But if Murtha gained nothing from that adventure, Finn was given two gifts that were to be very important to him in later days. When cooking the trout some hot fat had spluttered from the pan, burning his thumb. Afterward, when faced with a puzzle, all he had to do was put that thumb in his mouth, and the answer would float into his head.

One other thing came from burning himself in the fire of wisdom's recipe. The scorch was magical, and magicked Finn's hand in the presence of death. So that when anyone lay dying, or newly dead, Finn could revive the corpse by giving it water to drink out of his cupped hands. Such water would become, briefly, the water of life, and death would flee.

But this gift, like all Finn's gifts, was to cause him much trouble in time to come.

The Winter Burning

The King of Ireland lay asleep in his castle at Tara. Behind huge stone walls he slept, and the antechambers were full of armed men; even so, a dream slipped by and invaded his sleep. He was awakened by the sound of his own voice, bellowing. Sword in hand, the Royal Guards rushed in.

"I do not want you," said the king. "Here is a threat beyond violence. Send for my Druids."

The Druids came and the king told his dream.

"A young lad walks along a shore I have never seen, but I know it is near. His hair is so black it seems blue and his eyes so blue they look black. He is attended by a fish in armor and a tomcat larger than a terrier. He stops to look upon the skeleton of a whale. The wind blows through the ribs, making a battle music; the boy sings with it, sings words of menace and mirth as the waves dance and the fish jigs on his tail and the cat bows and the moon wobbles in a ghastly dance. Read me the dream then, O men of wisdom."

The Druids deliberated among themselves, beards wagging. The eldest spoke.

"Know this, High King, your dream is but the last in a series of signs that tell a doomful event—the coming of Finn McCool."

"The name means nothing to me."

"Finn McCool, son of Cuhal, leader of the Fianna, murdered by old Morna whose sons enjoy your favor."

"Son of Cuhal is he? And why was not the wolf-whelp killed along with his father?"

"His mother hid him."

"Was no search made?"

"High, low, over, under, middle, and across. But she hid him well."

"And was it young Finn I saw in my dream?"

"Himself. It was a prophetic dream you had—as the best kings do—so that you might prepare yourself."

"Does he dare come here so young and ungrown to avenge his father and claim the leadership of the Fianna?"

"He does so."

"Shall I fear a boy?"

"You shall. He has learned of the Salmon and knows things it is well for one's foe not to know. You must arm yourself, King. A living enemy has stepped out of the colored shadows of your sleep."

So the High King of Ireland prepared himself against the coming of Finn, and plotted deeply with the sons of Morna. Now by the Law of Hospitality the boy could not be killed while a guest at the castle, nor upon the road to it. The trick then would be to make him quit the court by his own choice, for the Law also said that a guest might not be forced to leave—but, once having left the king's table he was fair game and could be sent to join his father upon the unthawing ice fields that lie in the Darkness Beyond Night.

"What we must do is make him *want* to leave," said the king to Goll McMorna, eldest of the cruel beautiful sons of Morna.

"Well, let us think now," said Goll. "If he was tutored by the Salmon, he will know full well that he is protected by the Law of Hospitality, and will leave only if it becomes too uncomfortable for him to stay."

"The Law also says he cannot be forced to leave."

"Who speaks of forcing? We will merely introduce him to an experience or two that no lad of mettle would care to miss. If the sport becomes too rough, or an accident befalls—well, no blame can attach to us for we will have warned him."

"You speak in riddles, Goll. How can we warn him against danger and still lead him into it?"

"If he be son of Cuhal, O King, then he will be ridden by a pride that will gall him bloody when he shows fear. I remember well how his father spurred his gray stallion straight into our ambush, knowing that we couched there in our strength, but scorning to turn tail on a fight though he be outnumbered ten to one. Yes, if he be true son of Cuhal, our warnings will serve as joyous summons to a fatal task."

Castles then were not so grimly gray as they were later to become. The walls of Tara were cut out of a white cliff; its roof was striped crimson and blue. Chariots circled the walls, carrying two warriors each. They were drawn by matched stallions. Finn, seeing this blaze of color for the first time, forgot about his murdered father and his plans for vengeance and gawked joyously at the tall young charioteers whose yellow hair streamed in the speed of their going. And the magnificent war stallions took the rest of his breath, for if there was one thing Finn esteemed above another, it was a handsome animal—man, woman, dog, or horse.

As the lad stood staring at the bright chariots, a man strolled up holding a falcon, not on his wrist as falconers do, but perched on his shoulder. This pleased Finn because the man had a hawk face himself and it was like seeing a man with two heads. Now riding on Finn's shoulder was the Fish-hag's black tom, who accompanied the lad everywhere since breaking with the witch. The man looked down at the boy. The falcon glared down at the cat, who swelled with rage, arching his back and greening his eyes. Finn laughed.

"Something amuse you?" said the man.

"Much amuses me, sir," said Finn. "I am easily entertained."

"Are you now? But perhaps I do not care to be laughed at by a raw cub, whose name, estate, and parentage I do not know."

"My name is Finn McCool. I am my father's son, as will be disclosed to those who knew him last. As for my estate, this I must discuss with the High King."

"And do you think the High King can listen to every vagabond who turns off the road?"

"No, sir. But to Finn McCool, yes."

"Is there something special about you, Master McCool?"

"I cannot tell. I am the only one of me I know."

"I have the liveliest kind of wish to beat you until you cannot walk," said the tall man.

"I'm sorry to hear that," said Finn.

"You'd be sorrier yet, my lad, if you were not shielded by the Law of Hospitality."

"Seems a pity that a man like you should be balked by a little thing like a law," said Finn.

"Do not mock me," gritted the man.

"I know how you must feel not being able to beat me," said Finn. "I see that you are a man of splendid wrath. I see the flaming coils of it springing from your head."

Now it was a deadly insult at that time to refer to anyone's physical appearance, unless it were a lover, chieftain, or closest kin, or any combination of these. And Finn knew that he was walking a knife-edge. He was trying to provoke the man to attack, of course; for, without knowing the redhead's name, he had recognized him immediately as a final foe, whom he must either destroy or be destroyed by. And since he was too young to engage him in physical combat, Finn was trying to goad him into losing his temper and violating the Law of Hospitality, thus incurring the death penalty. This was Finn's plan, but, observing the man's face gone suddenly cheese-white, and the huge writhing fingers, Finn saw that he might have gone too far, that he might have let himself in for immediate annihilation, which was not part of his plan at all. For the boy had met enemies before—snakes and hags and all the sore magic blades in a witch's kit—but he had never yet angered mortal man, and he was amazed to see how totally savage was this wrath, lighted by intelligence, more urgent than hunger, closer than breathing.

The man said nothing at all; his fingers were playing now with the ankle gyve of the bird. The huge falcon rose suddenly from the man's shoulder, soared until it was blotted in the gray brightness, then dived. It dropped out of the sky in a heavy screaming stoop straight for Finn's head. Finn looked up. Gaffing down upon him were the huge hooks that could tear the heart out of an arctic goose in mid-flight. Bigger than the sky they came clutching for his head.

The cat on Finn's shoulder yawned, flicking its coral tongue, grinning right into the hooks of death—then rose straight up in a great leap to meet the dropping falcon. Finn watched aghast, expecting to see his pet, twice beloved because it was taken from an enemy, smashed into a bloody rag of fur. But he had forgotten that it was a witch's cat, witness to spells and incantations. The black tom uttered a rhymed meow, and made a delicate pass with its paws. Finn saw the falcon dwindle into a wren, which had time for but one flutter before the cat pulled it in, and, dropping back onto Finn's shoulder, began to chew.

"I would sooner have lost my stable of horses," said the man softly. "I took that hawk from the King of Aram after a fight that lasted three days and cost ten of my best men, not to mention a few of the worst. How shall I refrain from killing you where you stand despite all the Laws of Hospitality ever spoken by half-witted ancients?"

"I put you under Obligation," said Finn.

He said a word to the cat, who spat feathers which floated on the air, thickening into the royal shape of the falcon. The bird spread its huge wings briefly and resumed its perch on the man's shoulder.

"That's a clever cat you have there," said the man.

"He has had certain advantages," said Finn. "Now sir, I have told you my name, will you tell me yours?"

"Goll McMorna."

"How well things fall out. You are the man I most wanted to know, and I meet you first. You were the leader of those who killed my father, I believe."

"Still am."

"So I must kill you, of course."

"Of course you must try."

"But not quite yet. I need to grow to my full size first."

"You had better grow fast," said McMorna. "That Hospitality nonsense shelters you only while you are a guest here, and the Law of Obligation lasts only one year thereafter."

"Oh, but I may abide here quite a while. Tara's hospitality is famous."

"Yes, the king has been known to devise novel entertainments," said Goll. "Especially for uninvited guests. Come, I'll take you to him now."

The High King made Finn welcome. Stags were roasted whole in the great fireplaces of Tara, and young pigs, wood grouse, and pheasant turned on their spits, dripping hot gravy and giving off a smell that made the dogs howl with greed. Finn was questioned about his favorite dishes, and was served winter strawberries in clotted cream, hot chestnuts, honeycomb—and one night a fat trout cooked according to the recipe given him by the Salmon that night he had fed it to the Druids and stuffed them so full that he was able to make off with their secret wisdom.

"You need new clothes," said the king. "No son of Cuhal shall walk Tara clad like a peasant."

And he bade his tailor weave Finn a chestful of garments out of spiderweb, the lightest strongest thread in all the world, and they were dyed blue and rust and silver.

There was feasting every night. Bards sang stories, poets riddled, slave girls danced, acrobats turned, bears were baited, cocks fought. By day there was hunting and fishing and jousting, foot races, wrestling, puzzle-verse, chess, and bowls. And all during these first days of welcome Goll McMorna was at the king's right hand, devising pleasures for Finn.

One night at the feasting the king stood on the table, banging a gold dish with his dagger.

"Silence!" he cried. "I would speak."

The voices fell off. The huge dining hall filled with a silence so deep there seemed to be a humming at its core.

"Tonight is the Night of the Winter Burning," said the king. "Tonight we fortunate ones who dwell at Tara pay our yearly toll of shame and blame and flame. Tonight we are visited by the Destroyer, and a brave man will watch, and there will be peril and pain. I need a brave man now. Who offers himself? Any man here may volunteer save Goll McMorna whose chieftainship makes him exempt, and Finn McCool who is too young and tender for such an adventure, and is a guest besides. Speak then. Who dares watch through the fatal night?"

"I claim guest-gift," said Finn.

"What?" cried the king. "Now?"

"Even now."

"It is considered more courteous for a guest to take his gift when his visit ends."

"At the risk of discourtesy, O King, I must ask it now. Immediately. I cannot wait."

"What is it you wish then? If it lies within my bounty I must grant it."

"I wish to stand watch tonight against the Dread Coming."

"Impossible!"

"Entirely possible. It lies within your bounty."

"I need a strong man to stand against the Intruder. And even so, he will perish. But at least he will have made honorable resistance. You are but a lad with no experience in battle."

"Being young is an experience in itself," said Finn. "It has given me training in being outweighed, outnumbered, and—most advantageous of all in a conflict—underestimated."

Goll McMorna spoke: "It cannot be permitted, brave youth. It is certain death."

" 'Certain death' is a redundancy," said Finn. "Death is more certain than the royalty of kings, the stillness of stealth, the wisdom of good advice; it is, in fact, our prime certainty, and it is something that I, son of my father, have forbidden myself to consider. I ask your permission, King. Grant it, and you are quit of guest-gift."

"Will you allow me to watch with you?" said Goll McMorna.

"What? Challenge a foe, knowing myself backed by the strongest warrior in the realm? Where's the honor in that?"

All the men of the court sprang to their feet and cheered at the quickness and courtesy of his reply.

"Very well," said the king. "I have no choice. I must grant your request and make preparations for a noble wake."

Upon this night of the Winter Burning it seemed as if all the great world beyond the castle had gathered its weathers to contribute flame. The moon burned in the black sky, casting sparks that were stars. Water glittered in fen and tarn; slippery lights danced on the waves of the sea. Hayricks smoldered in the dark fields. The moonlight fell, now silver, now green, now gold, as it fractured variously from mown grass and copse and tangled field. Moonlight splintered upon the windows of Tara, and all the world was coldly aflame as Finn watched.

He was alone in the great council chamber. Everyone else had gone to sleep. Even the sentries had gone to sleep by order of the king, for none might await the Dread Coming save the Appointed Watcher. It was an enormous room Finn waited in. Here the king called his Druids and captains to make battle plan and to solve affairs of state. Here, although the boy did not know it, had Cuhal, his father, years before, taken the chieftainship of the Fianna. Weapons gleamed on the wall. The long thick lance used for the horse charge; the slender throwing javelin; the short handspear for the hedge-defense; the great two-edged sword for cutting and thrusting; the broad short swords of the ancient iron men, who, in the mists of memory had taken land to the east, slaughtered without pity, built roads, and vanished. Harpoons of the island fighters who used the same small spear for killing men and sticking great fish. Peasant weapons for working and fighting: pitchfork, sickle, scythe, mattock, pruning hook. Weapons taken from enemies: the curved new-moon swords and horn bows of the little slant-eyed men who rode small horses on beefsteak saddles—which were also their rations—and who devoured the land like a pestilence when they rode out of the rising sun; battle-axes and antlered helmets of the huge yellow-headed pirates who struck the coast like seahawks in their winged ships. And the enormous long swords that took two hands to swing, called claymores, belonging to the tall Picts in the north.

Finn gazed upon these weapons. He had never yet fought with weapons. His fingers itched to hold each one, to strike with it, and to add his own trophy to the loot upon the wall. He brooded upon the weapons. Each one, he knew, held a scroll of stories, of battle and death and brave intention. He wanted to know each story, and add his own. There among the weapons, like a swan among gulls, hung a harp, an ancient one by its shape. Locked in its strings, he knew, were the songs of these weapons and the men who had wielded them. By now he had almost forgotten about his mission that night and the Dread Coming. He kept staring at the harp. Each string was a thread of moonlight. The Thrig of Tone had taught him only pipe and lute, but as he stretched his fingers he could feel a current of story-music streaming between him and the harp. And then, amazed, he saw the harp slide along the weall. He dropped his hands and the harp stopped. Just as he was caught up in the delight of this, something said:

"Burn! Burn!"

He whirled toward the voice. He saw a tall cloaked figure looming blackly against the moon, which now looked in through the window in perfect fullness. The figure dropped its cloak. It was a woman. But difficult to see now for she was clad in a long tunic, moon-colored. Her eyes were two holes and her mouth was another. Her nose was a hole. And he felt his wits slipping as her hair shook for there was no distinction between the color of her hair and that of her face. He saw

that it was not hair at all, as we know it, but strands of skin with the power of movement. It moved upon her head, separating into tentacles of flesh that reached and curled, noosing the attention, as a snake, weaving, charms a bird so it cannot move.

"Stand!" said Finn. "Name yourself. And your errand here."

"I come to burn," she said. "I am she who comes by night to parch all moist ideas of youth, to devour honor and courage and all their ornaments and implements, and finally, most cruel, to incinerate hope itself by my punctuality. For men know that I must come and come again upon the night, and no matter what they do or what they say or how they grieve or how they pray, they cannot stay my coming. Queen of Crones am I, marrow of death, come to teach the nature of flame. What is it, young man? You like riddles. What is flame? Give me its name."

Finn said nothing. He was trying to escape the mesh of that weaving hair. Trying to struggle out of the spell cast by that voice and the words it said.

"You do not know? Then I shall teach you. Fire is impatience, deadliest of sins. Fire is despair galloping. Fire is the inevitable summoned too soon in the secret craven hollow of men, who, in their vile fear of What-Must-Be bring it on too early to ease the pain. Fire is impatience. Fire is death dancing, the music of chaos, the jewel of waste. See?"

From all the holes of her face flame gushed. Fire spurted yellow, red, and green. Tapestries burst into flame. The draft of the flame moved the weapons on the wall, making them chime, touched the string of the harp, which uttered one moaning syllable like a strong man in unutterable pain. She spat at the huge oaken council table, which fell into ash.

Then, most horrible, he saw the tentacles that were her hair coil upon themselves, then violently uncoil, springing clear off her head and hissing through the air toward him. He snatched a sword from the wall and flailed the air, cutting the tentacles into pieces as they came. Each piece, as it fell to the floor, became a fleshy worm with a torch in its tail. The fiery army inched toward him as their mistress harried them onward, screaming out of her mouth-hole.

Finn could not defend himself. There was no use striking with his sword. The tentacles were cut as fine as could be. They swarmed up his legs, stinging him with their fiery tails. In his agony he sang the Final Rune taught him by the Salmon.

> Creature pair of earth and air,
> Here and there and everywhere—
> Come, I pray, and serve me fair.

No sooner had he sung that than he saw his black tomcat leap into the room. Half-blinded by smoke, he saw the great gray falcon of Goll McMorna stoop for the kill, claws gaping. Cat and hawk moved through the fiery worms like mowers through a field, slashing with tooth and claw, sweeping the meaty little gobbets into their jaws, flame and all, screaming the proud scream of rage consuming its object, growing with all it fed upon.

But the ordeal had only begun. Still confronting Finn was the tall robed figure of his enemy, bald now, her head pocked with scorch marks, closer now. He heard the soft wordless crooning of her hate. She smiled at him. An arrow of flame seared his head and buried itself in the oaken bench, which flared brightly, fell to ash. She moved toward him. The front of his shirt caught fire.

All the contrariness of Finn gathered itself in a cold coil in his chest, freezing his flesh. He summoned up the loveliest, coldest images his short life had known: icy fire of cat's-eye, blue shadow of snow, turquoise wink of mountain lake, wind made visible being clothed in mist, silhouette of Fish-hag against the yellow moon, a tatter of crows, chatter of bats at dusk, hard shark-smile of Norah's Shoal, and, finally, the chill tinkle of Murtha's laughter when she wanted him to know that he needed to be scorned. The cold images clustered like snow crystals, shielding him from the darts of fire. The crone, thwarted, screamed a huge gout of flame that rolled across the floor, charring away planks, eating the beams down to the foundation stone. The floor tottered, and the whole castle spun upon its axis, whirling its shadows, scattering moonlight like the jeweled fire-tops that pampered princelings play with in the Land beyond the Sun.

Finn fell to his knees, sinking beneath the heat of that hateful flame that was burning away his crystal shield. He stretched his arms toward Dagda's harp, the harp of the ancients, which hung on Tara's wall and had once belonged to the wizard bard of the Tuatha da Danaan, who sang the beginning of things, the roots of heaven and earth, in the days when the gods dawned upon the unpeopled world.

The harp flew through the air, into Finn's arms. Cradling it, he played one icy plangent note, and released it. The harp flew as easily through flame as the Phoenix, that marvelous bird who lives in the heart of fire and is reborn from ash, and has become the sign of man's hope. Through net of flame flew the harp, singing icily, straight at the crone and smote her so hard that her head was torn from her shoulders and was hurled through the window, spouting blood and flame.

The window smashed and was glued by her blood, retaining the color of flame. Lozenges of moonlight fell upon the splintered floor, healing its planks. All things arose again from the ash as Finn cradled the harp and sang the phoenix-song, sang each weapon and its numbered battles, which he learned through his fingers as he sang, for the harp played him even as he played it. Song of battle and deed and death, the colored fountains of hope, and the parching of age. Sang past his own memory of how his father had won the chieftainship of the Fianna from the arrogant beardless youth who was now the twisted old king. And of how he, Finn, his father's son, come unto radiant triumph after the night of ordeal, would claim his own chieftainship, and begin that scroll of deeds that would become song, sung perhaps by his own son when it would be his time to sing.

The tomcat bounded in wearing scorched fur, angry, its eyes spitting green fire, and leaped upon Finn's shoulder to be comforted.

The great gray falcon flew in, feathers singed, squawking a huge oath of vengeance upon everything that moved beneath the sky, and sat on Finn's other shoulder. She and the tom were inseparable now. She had left Goll, and belonged to Finn.

And Finn, observing them, smiled to himself, remembering what the harp had told him—that he would have to take a bird and break a spell of the McMorna before they would be allowed to fight each other to the death.

The Scroll
of Debts

The next morning Finn lay asleep after his adventure with the Lady of the Winter Burning. As he slept, the High King spoke secretly to Goll McMorna.

"Our young friend has done what no man of us could do," said the king. "I am put under heavy bonds of obligation."

"Softly," said Goll. "He has done well so far—even very well perhaps—but his victories have been deeds of magic, not might. While I do not belittle this unsavory aptitude, still I cannot help associating it with witches and wizards and Druids and such rather than with men of high courage and good mettle."

"All very well," said the king. "But winning is winning and losing is losing. I have done both and I know. Only failure needs explanation. Success is its own argument. This boy has weathered the Dread Coming and saved Tara from burning. He has earned any gift within my power. Undoubtedly he will claim his father's place, which you now hold."

"He has earned any gift within *your* power," said Goll, "but the chieftainship of the Fianna is not yours to give. Do not forget that the Fianna is a band of unique warriors, the most skillful in all the green world, and that their chief must be the best among them. Even to become the least of this band—an honor sought by every lad in Eire—the candidate, buried to the waist, and armed only with hazel stick and wicker shield, must be able to defend himself against the attack of nine warriors fully armed. Next, having defeated the nine warriors, and pulled himself from the hole, he must braid up his hair and run like a fox with the Fianna in full cry after him. Through all the woods and fields of Eire must he run, from sea to sea. And, if he is caught, or if a twig snaps under his foot, or one strand of his hair be disarrayed in its shining braid, then that lad has failed and will never be admitted to our number. Several other small tasks he is set: to jump from a standing position over a stick held level with his brow; to run full-speed carrying sword, shield, and spear under that same stick held at the height of his knee; to run barefoot over a field of nettles; to step full upon one, and receive the thorn driven into his foot without outcry or murmur of pain, then, hopping, and without losing speed, to remove that thorn from his foot, and so proceed over the field. Until our lad can perform these trifles he will be less than the least of us, let alone qualified to be our chief. Magic alone won't do it, nor a gift of song, nor a trick of words. By weapons we live, by the death of our enemies do we prosper, by spear-shock, sword-thrust, mail-denting blow of fist, by kick that can shatter walls. By stealth of dagger, swiftness of arrow, blunt argument of club—and, above all, by that delight in battle which can transform the bloodiest encounter into pleasant hours, the meatiest murder into food for jest. Without this transforming joy in carnage, which is the warrior's magic, without it, I say, O King, the lad will never be our chief. He may have it, but he has to prove it."

The king stroked his beard. He called his Druids to council.

Long they sat, and the tapers burned, and the fireplaces were blazing against the chill of night before the king was ready to receive Finn.

When the boy came into the throne room he was greeted by a great shout of welcome. All the court and its ladies pressed about him. The men buffeted him with blows of congratulation; the ladies put their perfumed arms about him and bestowed upon him the kiss of victory. By the time he stood before the throne he was rosy with pleasure. The very shadows seemed to be dancing in celebration, and the world and its ways sat very sweet upon him.

The king rose and came down from his throne, a sign of high courtesy.

"You have brought us safely through the Winter Burning. We at Tara, appointed by the gods to guide the destinies of Eire, do thank you. Through us all the people of our domain thank you. Now, Finn McCool, you must know that this deed has put us under Bond of Obligation. You may ask whatever lies in my power to bestow."

"Great King, kind host, I am grateful for your words. There is nothing I would claim save that which I would have asked my father had he lived—the chieftainship of the Fianna."

The buzz of voices fell away. Laughter ceased. Every belted man and every green-clad lady turned eyes away from Finn to look upon Goll McMorna, who stood, as always, at the king's right hand. The silence thickened.

Goll McMorna spoke in a quiet, pleasant voice. "That which you ask is not in the king's power to give. The Fianna is a band of uniquely endowed and uniquely trained fighting men who have banded together by their own free choice. They make their own rules, select their own chief, and serve what king they will. It is a long road to the chieftainship. First you must become a member of the band, and to do that you must perform those initiation rites which so many have failed. Then you must so acquit yourself in battle and in council that each Fenian would have you for his leader, and no other. Finally, you must dispose of the existing chief—who happens to be myself."

Finn bowed courteously, and said:

"When I was a babe in my bullhide cradle, O Goll, I was lulled to sleep not by nursery rhymes but by war songs of the Fenians. Yes, I heard my father sing. He put all the initiation rites to rhyme, and all the battles. And when I finally fell asleep it was to dream of these things and myself doing them. As for the feats of qualification, I can perform all, I believe, except fending off the onslaught of nine warriors and myself buried to the waist. But when I come to my full growth I hope to be able to do that also. Then, having been accepted into the Fianna, all else shall happen as happen may. And if my youth be crowned by the great honor of killing you, O killer of my father and valuable tutor of myself, perhaps indeed will I assume my place under the sign of glory."

"There is a further thing I should mention," said Goll McMorna. "No man may enter the Fianna until he settles all unpaid debts—not only those owed by himself, but those his father may have incurred."

"I have no such debts," said Finn.

"You have inherited a few—nine of them, in fact."

Then Finn, teased at last out of his temper, raised his voice in challenge. "If there be any man here with unsettled claim against my father, let him stand forth now, and I shall erase either debt or creditor."

"Softly," said Goll. "I will explain these debts. There is a rule of the Fianna that says no request for aid may go unanswered, especially if it means a fight against odds. Whenever anyone comes a-crying about oppressor or foe or monster too fearsome for ordinary man to handle, why then we are pleased to attend to the matter at no fee. Now, according to our rule, that obligation is incurred personally by the chief himself. He may dispatch any man he pleases upon this errand, but he himself owes the deed until it is done. As it happened, there were some requests unfulfilled when your father met his abrupt

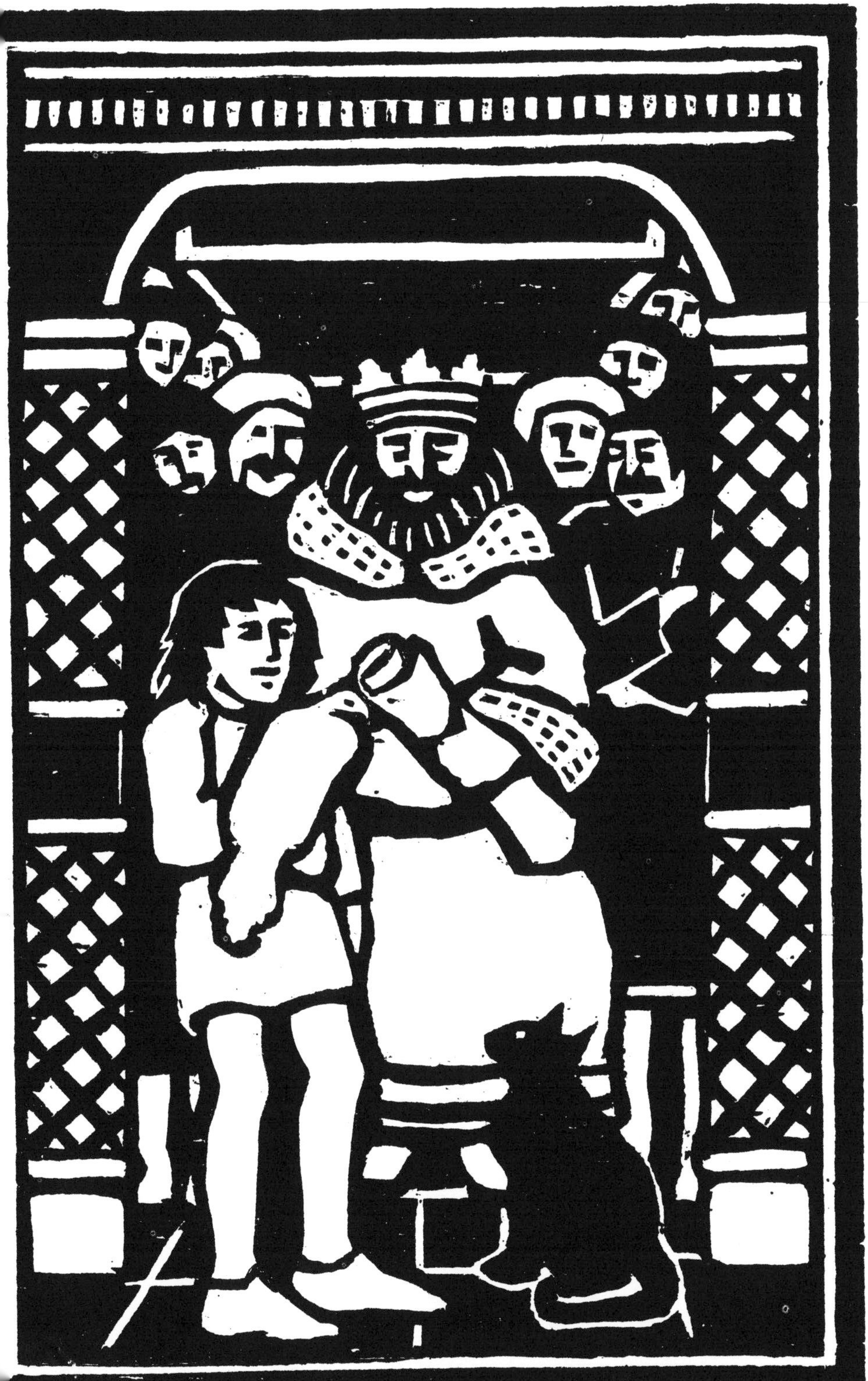

demise, and for one reason or another certain of these deeds are still undone. You, Finn, as your father's heir, are responsible. I, as chief of the Fianna, proclaim now that no man of us will discharge any of these tasks, but will, in all generosity, allow you your chance to show what you can do. Until these deeds are done you cannot qualify for membership in our band."

Finn looked about. The huge hall which had been so warm, so full of friends, now seemed a cold, empty place. The faces which had been all admiration and smiles were now the blank ones you see in time of trouble. He looked at the king. The old face was like a stone now with a mossy beard. He looked at Goll, whose hawk face was split by a smile of malice.

He said: "I have been ignorant of these things."

"It was an obscure rule," said Goll, "never invoked until now, to be sure, but everything must begin somewhere, must it not?"

"What are these deeds I owe?"

"They make an interesting list," said Goll.

He handed Finn a scroll; the lad unrolled it.

"Read them aloud," said Goll. "I'm sure everyone wishes to hear what projects will attract your valiant efforts in the years that lie ahead."

Finn read the words of the scroll so that all might hear.

> THE LION OF LOUTH
> THE BLUE SWORD
> THE IRON STAG
> HOULIHAN'S BARN
> THE MARES OF MUNSTER
> THE FIRE-BULL
> THE APPLES OF ARLA
> THE WITCH-DOG OF WEIR
> THE BOAR OF BALLINOE.

When he had finished reading, Finn stared Goll full in the face and said in a loud clear voice:

"Paying those debts will keep me busy a long while. I'm sure you regret as much as I do that our mortal combat must be postponed."

Now this remark of Finn's was as good as accusing Goll of cowardice before all the court—which is the way Finn wanted him to take it. And the lad rejoiced to see his enemy's face flush purple and his coiled red hair spit flame. But Goll did not lose control. He took a deep breath, and said:

"We do not wish to be ungenerous. Therefore, by consent of the Fianna you will be allowed to return to Tara and challenge me for the chieftainship after completing but three of these labors, the remaining debts to be paid in the years of your full manhood, if, by some miracle, you live to see them."

"Any three?" said Finn.

"Any three. They are all beyond your strength, I fear. So choose what three you will. And, if you should succeed, come back to Tara, young Finn, and you and I will fight in single combat for the leadership of the Fianna which I killed your father to gain, and stand ready to do as much for the son."

"Thank you, Goll," said Finn. "I trust I shall know how to repay your generosity when the time comes. Thank you, King, for your hospitality. Thank you all, sirs and ladies, for wit and beauty and courtesy. Farewell now. I will return after doing the third deed."

So saying, he left the throne room, and the castle.

The Boar
of Ballinoe

F inn set out from Tara on the coldest day in memory. The trees were clothed in ice, and a single sheet of ice stretched as far as he could see. A flight of wild geese, honking like hounds, froze solid in mid-flight and fell into the bay without losing its V-shape, making a great splash that froze into a net of ice as the boy watched, amazed.

He was surprised at himself too. For here he was driven from the comforts of Tara, from its blazing fireplaces and roasting meats and warm-breathed perfumed ladies, out into this flaying wind to seek out the most fearsome creatures whose names were ever whispered—and instead of being miserable, he was bursting with wild joy. The weak sunlight fractured off the icy trees in a dance of light. He saw fiery splinters of blue, purple, red, green, yellow, white, blue, paler blue, storm-pink lilac, and the purples of wrath—the crystal trees bore fire-fruit where the sun touched them. And bending in the wind and shaking their boughs, they made a tinkling ice-music for light to dance by.

He did not feel the cold. He was clad in fur of wolf and bear he had killed himself, and he was busy trying to decide which adventure to seek first. The order of things is very important when you are moving among the brute order of events—which is always—and if you seek the aid of magic, then the sequence of words and numbers is also most meaningful. He decided to consult the Salmon of Knowledge.

He could not, of course, consult the actual Salmon himself, who lay locked in unknown leagues of ice deep under some mountain stream, so he did what the Salmon had told him to do in such an event—he bit the thumb which he had burned when cooking the Loutish Trout according to recipe. He bit his thumb, and said:

> Salmon, Salmon, I bite my thumb.
> Speak ye forth, be not dumb.
> Come to me this day of ice
> With fish-mouth words of wise advice.

As he spoke, the words themselves froze in the air and fell to earth, rearranging their letters and spelling out new words. This is what he read:

> Yes of foe
> Always no.
> In such a test
> first is worst
> last is best.

"Thank you, Salmon," said Finn aloud. Then to himself: "Now, what can he mean?"

He read the verse and read it again. But still it made no sense. "I can't ask him, either," said Finn to himself. "He will never repeat himself nor ever explain. He teaches that the best part of wisdom is unriddling things for yourself. I did pretty well at such puzzles when I was under his tutelage, but my wits have grown rusty, I fear, at Tara. Still, I *must* make myself understand. For ignorance, upon the start of such a journey, is death's own darkness."

He stared at the words again, and stared and stared, sunk upon his haunches, feeling the very marrow of his bones freeze as the wind screamed.

Finn heard something. He whirled about and looked back toward the castle and saw a remarkable sight—Dagda's harp flying after him. Its strings were tightened by the cold, and it sang as it flew:

> Farewell Tara's halls
> Its weaponed walls.
> I journey long
> to aid your song.

"Would you be coming with me then?" asked Finn in wonder. "O Harp of Dagda, will you accompany this homeless lad upon a scroll of deeds?"

The harp answered:

> Who fingers my strings
> full sweetly sings
> of colored shadows, truthful lies,
> of the fears of the brave
> and the folly of the wise.

"Ah, you rhyme after my own heart!" cried Finn. "Unriddle me this verse then."

> Yes to foe
> Always no.
> In such a test
> first is worst
> last is best.

"This is the message sent me by the Salmon of Knowledge, a most wise and prophetic fish. Can you read me its meaning?"

"I can," said the harp.

> I tell you, Finn
> brave young friend,
> Your tasks begin
> At the very end.

"Begin at the end, is it? But is this indeed what he means—that I must start at the last item, the Boar of Ballinoe instead of the Lion of Louth, which heads the list?"

"Yes, yes, so I guess," sang the harp.

> Not north to Louth
> But west by south
> Must we go
> toward Ballinoe.

"West by south it is!" cried Finn. "And ho to the Boar of Ballinoe!"

The cat and falcon, too dark against the snow, found the hunting very poor. Finn consulted the harp and was taught a spell:

> Cat and bird
> By this word
> I teach you to bleach
> Quite out of sight.
> Now each by each
> Go white, go white.

No sooner had he said this spell than the cat turned white as an ermine, and the feathers of the gray falcon paled until she disappeared against the snow, except for the hot black circles of her eyes. Invisible to their prey, then, cat stalked and hawk stooped, and filled their bellies again.

After some whirling snowy miles Finn met a man in rusty armor riding the skeleton of a horse; his hands were bone and his head a skull. He offered combat, but Finn said:

"Begone! I cannot wound you for you have no blood. I cannot kill you for you are dead."

The wind whistled through the standing bones of the horse, making a thin laughter. The skull spoke:

"I was fat, very fat. My wife, the beauty, said: 'Stop eating. Grow thin, or I take a lover.' So I began to fast until I had starved myself quite away and became as you see me now. But she took a lover anyway because I was poor company at mealtime."

"Unjust, unjust!" cried Finn.

"All of that, brave lad. Even worse—for now, having grown fat by eating what I did not, she held profundity of flesh a virtue, said the body was a reflection of the soul, and that my soul must need be pinched and mean to produce such emaciation."

"Never have I heard such wicked reasoning," said Finn. "Did you kill her then?"

"Oh no, I loved her. I stayed on listening to her abuse, trying to be friendly with her lover—a stout man without much to say for himself—until she found that irksome too and bade me leave. So I found a horse to suit me, and must ride its whistling bones up and down the land until I find a man whose wife is a bigger bitch than mine. Then we two must fight a fight that is very pure, being only for rage and amusement and honor, you know, because it will be Winner Take Nothing. Are you the one, lad? Is your wife as fair and foul as mine?"

"I am a bachelor, sir."

"Then curse you! Ride on!"

"I am walking, as you see."

"Don't be wasting my time, bachelor. Walk on—before I smite you from sheer spite."

Some miles farther on, as they were climbing a low hill they saw a huge snowball rolling down the slope toward them, growing as it came. They gave it room to pass, but were amazed to see it pause on the slope, something very difficult for a snowball to do. A voice sounded:

"A question, young traveler."

"Ask away," said Finn. "I've never held converse with a snowball before, but I see nothing against it."

"You are a sweet cautious lad. But I'm getting quite chilled despite the warmth of my temperament. Won't you dig me out?"

Finn drew his sword and hacked away the snow.

"Gently now. I cut easily."

He plied his sword with care, scraping away the snow, until he came to the core of the matter. It was a woman, so fat that she rolled instead of walked, and, upon such a day, had gathered snow. She was red-faced and red-haired with a gurgling laugh.

"Thank you, young sir. Have you seen a man on a horse which is the very match of him, both being but skin and bone?"

"Nothing but bone, madame. I saw no skin."

"Ah, poor fellow, he does not prosper without my care. Which way did he go?"

"He wasn't going. He was staying. Waiting until another husband might pass whom he would challenge to prove who was Champion of Misfortune."

"He said harsh things about me, no doubt?"

"He did that. But I know there are two sides to every quarrel."

"Two? There are ten! Twenty perhaps. In fact, a real quarrel between husband and wife has no sides at all; it's perfectly round, just like me. Tell me, what is your own preference? Do you care only for those meager little sparrow-girls, or might you fancy perhaps a woman of substance?"

"I have had slight experience of women, fat or thin. I grew up with a girl named Murtha whom I simply cannot describe. I don't know what I like."

"Then roll along with me, lad. We'll gather snow enough to hide us from prying eyes, and I shall teach you what to like."

"Dear lady," said Finn. "I am enchanted by every degree of your luscious rotundity. Lucky the man who can play radius to your circumference. Unfortunately, I am on a mission and may not tarry."

"Pity," said the lady. "Then I must go looking for my husband, I suppose."

"Just follow the road, and you will find him."

Now upon this winter so weirdly cold that the sea froze, fur-hatted men swarmed down from the Land of the Long Night, swooping across the ice on narrow sleds that bore mast and sail, and outraced the north wind. Seagulls spotted these invaders while they were still far north of Eire, and screamed the news from flock to flock. The falcon heard the tale as it was striking a heron, and flew back to tell the cat.

"That is a large bird you bring, brother," said the tom. "Is it tough as it looks?"

"It is meat, brother, and hard to find these frosty days. Have you killed?"

"Only a limping hare. Everything one can eat seems to be hiding in its hole waiting for the thaw. There will be much hunger this winter."

"Worse than famine is abroad," said the falcon. "The Seal-clad Ones of the Place Beyond the Mist are coming over the frozen seas. In sheeted sleds they come, and the smell of blood comes with them. Yea, I smell battle, brother, and much slaughter. Let us welcome it. We hawks deem it shameful to eat what we do not kill, but it is sometimes necessary. I do not relish man-flesh, except for their eyeballs, which are sweet when fresh. In this weather they should keep for days."

"You have disgusting habits," hissed the cat. "Were we not under magic bonds of friendship, I should seek to express my disapproval more sharply."

"Dear little caterpillar," cooed the falcon. "You are too furry and earthbound to threaten me. Let us put aside our friendship for a bit and debate my habits with tooth and claw."

"It cannot be," said the cat. "We are on a hero's venture—we are Companions of the Doom. We must not indulge in private quarrels. Accept my apologies."

"Accepted," said the falcon.

"Go on with your tale. Are they such fearsome warriors, these Seal-clad Ones?"

"They carry fish-spears that can pierce the leather armor of that behemoth they call the whale, also walrus-tusk swords. And they are very hungry. Also they come so swiftly that they will attack before anyone knows they are here. But what if they fail? Then they will be dead, and *their* eyeballs will be eaten."

"We must hold fast to our master and protect him in the time of fighting," said the cat. "I wish him alive. He saved me from the Hag, and I am grateful."

"I am a war falcon, as you know. Trained by Goll McMorna to stoop upon warriors as well as game. And, as I say, I prefer to eat only what I kill. So I am yours to command, O hag-free and spell-spitting tom."

Finn, who was plucking the heron for their supper, heard the cackles and mewing of this conversation, and was amazed to find himself understanding it. But the hawk's tale was so strange that he thought it might be happening in his own head.

"Do I understand them?" he asked the harp.

"You do."

"But how?"

"Through me. I am the Harp of Dagda, who was the most potent bard of the Tuatha da Danaan, and, as you see, I am strung with catgut instead of wire. And at that time, you must know, cats were big as cows—which was as well, for rats were big as rams. You understand the tom then through me, and through him the speech of other beasts and birds, but only so long as you carry me and touch my strings."

"Then it is true that sailing sleds speed toward these shores?"

"Too true. And there will be great slaughter when they come. They used to strike these coasts long ago, in the days when Dagda was first learning his scales, and he lived two thousand years, did my sweet master, before he was cut down in his prime. The seas were always frozen then, and the Seal-clad Ones would strike by night in their winged sleds, and kill and kill and kill. But then the sea gods fought. Lyr and Tyre fought their deep duel and left each other wounded on the floor of the sea. And the blood from their huge bodies, always flowing and always warm—for gods cannot die, only bleed—heated the seas and kept them from freezing, melting the ice plains and forming an impassable gulf of waters for the Seal-clad ones. Until now . . . until now."

"And we are the only ones who know of this coming?"

"We alone."

"What shall I do?"

> Build man of snow
> Let the winds blow.

Finn struck camp immediately and did not bed down for the night, but worked until dawn, raising a giant man of snow. In its eyeholes he stuffed tufts of rabbit fur soaked in oil of the heron's liver, and put fire to them. The snow giant, looming on its headland, glared with enormous burning eyes over the frozen sea. In its lifted hand he balanced a young pine, and it seemed to be poised to cast a huge spear. He had placed the snow giant so that it faced north by west, and the north wind howled at an angle into its earhole and out its westering mouth, making a terrible sobbing bellowing cry.

You can still see that giant if you find the headland. It stands there where Finn built it in one night, but the snow has turned to white stone, and its legs and trunk are one column of stone. Its eye-holes are dead. But you may know it by its raised arm and by the sobbing bellowing sound it still makes when the wind blows strongly off the North Sea.

But it served its purpose for Finn that night so long ago. The fur-hatted invaders did not strike the coast of Eire, and the bards say it was because they feared the giant standing sentinel on the headland, and its burning eyes and the shadow of its mighty spear, and they imagined Eire a land of giants. Be that as it may, we do know that the next day was even colder, so cold that the sunset froze in the sky. Its weight overbalanced the horizon, and it slid down the tilted line of the sky to the North Pole, where it stuck, flashing there in a pageantry of frozen colors we call the Northern Lights.

"Quickly!" said the harp. "Visit the sunset before it slides away and search its roots for the seeds of fire."

"Why?"

"You will need them. Go!"

Finn bound long straight branches to his feet like the runners of a sled. He slung his sword belt to the falcon, who seized one end of it in her beak and drew Finn swiftly over the icy plain of the sea to the great frozen lake of flame. He felt small as a speck of dust, did Finn, when he came to the base of that pulsing radiant wall of color. Cold light poured down, staining him with its rich dyes, and his blood sang at the loveliness. The falcon flew slowly, pulling him on his skis past arches and columns and ramparts of living color to the red roots of the sunset. He dug there with his knife and pried out the seeds of fire, white-hot little pearls of the primal flame, which sprout with unbelievable speed when planted, and will nourish life or spread death according to the manner of their sowing, and must be handled only by heroes. He put the white-hot little pearls in his wallet and skied swiftly away as the sunset's weight began to tilt the horizon.

Now Finn turned from the coast and made his way southwest toward Ballinoe, for that was where his first task lay—to kill the boar that was ravaging the countryside. But the going was not easy. The weather had shifted suddenly. The iron frost was broken. A thaw set in, melting the snow, cracking the ice, turning the whole countryside into water. Freshets of water came tumbling off the hills. The rivers were enormously swollen, and overflowed their banks, washing away huts, barns, trees. Finn, passing, saw people afloat on their roofs. He saw cows swimming, and sheep and goats, all herded by dogs who paddled after, barking furiously. Roads were washed out, trees were uprooted. As far as the eye could see, the fields were covered with water. Finn hauled in a drifting coracle, and packed himself in it with cat and harp and falcon, and simply let his little boat go with the tide. The cat rode his shoulder, trying to fluff his wet fur, eyes burning disapproval at the idea of wetness. The falcon rode the bow, hunching malevolently between her wings. She, too, disliked the weather.

By and by as the sun came up warmly each morning, the waters shrank back off the fields. The land steamed. Dogs herded cattle back to the barns. Horses ran in the field, trumpeting. The road appeared again. Finn left his little boat and resumed his journey by foot.

The falcon flew high, searching for game. The cat stalked the underbrush. Finn strode on, hair loose in the wind, breathing deeply

of the wild moist air, now and again touching his harp. He came finally to Ballinoe, where he met an old woman on the road.

"Good day, Grandmother," he said. "And a good afternoon to
follow, and a good night after that. My name is Finn McCool."

"Is it now?"

"Do you dislike strangers here?"

"We do, but not so much as we dislike our neighbors."

"Is the place full of sadness and suspicion then, stewing in spite
and black looks and sour words? Is that the way of it?"

"It is. We are no different from anyplace else."

"But are you plagued by a wild boar?"

"Good day to you," said the woman. "I can't stand here talking
of this and that." She humped off rapidly down the road, muttering to
herself.

A while later Finn came to an inn. He entered and ordered a
meal.

"You look like a lad with a sharp appetite," said the landlord.
"What do you care to commence with, fish or fowl?"

"Why . . ."

"Don't give too much thought to it because we have neither.
Perhaps you would care to choose between plovers' eggs and carp
roe."

"Will I be served what I choose?"

"Well, that takes care of the first course," said the landlord.
"Now for the big decision. Will you have joint of beef, leg of lamb,
side of veal, or mutton chop?"

"You jest with me," said Finn. "There is no savor of food here.
Your kitchen fires are cold. Why do you mock a hungry man, innkeeper?"

"What else should I do to one who comes ordering a meal where
there is no food?"

"Why is there no food?"

"Because it has been eaten. We had a visitor before you, and he took it all. Carp, salmon, trout. Twenty dozen of plover eggs. A pail of roe. And six sheep, three cows, two goats, five kids—oh, and the lambs, of course, all ten. Flesh, fat, bone, muscle, sinew, skin and horn."

"Quite a feeder," said Finn. "But why such a long face, my host? And so sour a greeting for your next guest? If he emptied your larder, he filled your purse."

"Not he," growled the innkeeper. "He skinned me clean, you young fool. It was Boru the Bad who visited this inn and destroyed both peace and profit. He does not pay, man, he takes. Takes without giving. I'm lucky he did not eat my wife and children as well. Or perhaps not. For I don't know how I shall keep them now without cattle or grain or fish in the pond. No. It were better we were all dead than visited by Boru."

"What manner of man is he to look at?"

"Man? God save us. He is no man, but an ogre. Foul, friend, foul. Huge and foul. So ugly you sicken with it. So savagely strong you melt with fear. And of vile odor."

"What does he look like so that I will know him if I meet him?"

"If you meet him, my lad, you'll know him all right, but you won't be knowing anything for long. Avoid him is my advice."

"What does he look like?"

"So tall he has to bend almost double to squeeze through that door there, and about as wide as he is tall. With a fat face and little poisonous red eyes. A big snout on him, lad, a beard made of black bristles—and, look you, most horrible, two teeth, if you can call them teeth, but they come curving out of his mouth as long and sharp as the horns of an Angus bull."

"And does he terrorize the countryside?"

"He does not tranquilize it, that's for certain."

"Then he must be the wild boar they speak of in Tara."

"Well, his name is Boru, sure enough. And he does resemble a giant pig, now that you mention it. But if you heard of him, why are you here?"

"To cut short his career, my good host."

"You?"

"Myself and no other. Finn McCool."

"Finn the Fool, more likely."

"Careful now. You are an unfortunate man. Disaster has just struck you. I do not wish to strike you too. But do not play with my name."

The innkeeper looked at him a long time. He was a big enough fellow himself with a beefy face and great slabs of forearms, and a bullhide apron. Finn looked back at him. Finally, the man said:

"If you have come to fight Boru, I must wish you well."

"Thank you, master landlord. And good day to you."

Now, as Finn walked along the road he stopped each passerby and asked him what he knew about Boru. But he could learn nothing. Their faces closed when he spoke to them. They faced him sullenly, lips clenched, eyes clouded. "Why, they are frightened," he said to himself. "Too much afraid of this fellow even to mention his name— so far gone, so sunk in terror, they dare not serve their own interests." And he felt their fear begin to infect him, and was immediately shaken by the dancing rage that took him whenever he began to know fear. On impulse he stopped a small boy who passed, grinning.

"Why do you smile at me, young sir?"

"You're a funny sight you are, master stranger, with that cat on one shoulder and that ugly bird on the other."

"Would you earn a penny?"

"Rather be given one, but I'll earn it if there is no other way."

"Tell me then, have you heard of him called Boru?"

"Boru the Bad? Why, everyone has heard of him. He is the worst of living things, they say—and he lives right here in Ballinoe."

"Where?"

"And I shall be like him when I grow up and everyone shall fear me. I'm practicing wickedness right now. For you can't start early enough if you wish to make something of yourself, I am told."

"Where does Boru live?"

The boy grinned at him.

"Don't you want the penny?"

"Price has gone up. Twopence now."

Finn reached out and lifted him off the ground and held him upside down, kicking and yelping.

"Easy now, little merchant, or I shall drop you square on your scheming red head, and it will break like an egg. A penny I said, and a penny it shall be. Penny is the fee."

"Down this road, round the bend, up the hill and down again. Over a valley, across a stream—and there you will see a tall hill. That is his castle."

"He lives in the hill, does he?"

"Aye, he has hollowed it out. It is his stronghold, and there he lives, with his troops. And I hope you do find him, that's all I hope. But pay me my penny first. For you won't be around to collect any debts from, not after you meet Boru; no, that you won't."

Finn set the boy on his feet and gave him a penny.

"Now be off with you, little rascal, before I warm your tail."

The boy scampered off, cursing. Finn laughed, and went his way.

He went the way the boy had told him, and after a bit came to the stream. More river than stream, it was swollen to twice its size, and the current ran swiftly. Beyond the stream he could see the hollow hill that was Boru's castle.

"Looks like an ordinary hill to me," said Finn to himself. "Nevertheless, I believe that red-headed little liar for some reason, so there it is I shall go to seek Boru. I see no gate nor portal nor any means of entrance, but if he dwells there with his troops there must be a way in. First, however, I must cross this overgrown stream."

Now at this time there were few bridges that crossed the waterways of Eire, and those only along the most traveled routes. Ferries too were very scarce. It was the custom to cross water on stilts. On the bank of river or stream opposite a dwelling, there was always a stack of stilts for travelers to use. Just as Finn was selecting a pair, the harp spoke to him, saying:

> Walk on two spears
> And have no fears.

Now, as it happened, Finn carried no spear because he had wished to travel light. He was armed only with sword and dagger. But he had learned that the harp's advice was not to be ignored. So he cut two long thick branches. To one of them he bound his sword, to the other his dagger. Then to each he nailed a chock of wood to keep his feet on. Stepping very carefully, he edged into the stream.

All this time Finn was being watched by Boru from his barrow-castle. It was Boru's custom to attack travelers while they were crossing the stream. He would wait until they were midway, where the current was strongest, then rush into the stream, where he could move about much more quickly, for his legs were so long he needed no stilts. Then he would carry his catch off to the slave pens. Or, if the victim was fat and tasty-looking, he would find himself turning on a spit. Boru ate human flesh too.

But Finn knew nothing of all this as he stilt-walked across the tumbling stream. He had a difficult time of it, balancing himself against the current, nor was the task made any easier by his stilts being knife-tipped according to the harp's instruction. But he managed

all the same until he reached midstream. Then, suddenly, he heard a wild bellowing and snorting, and saw something huge and terrible splashing toward him from the other shore. A sight to make a strong man's courage melt away it was. According to O'Hare's *Book of Harms:*

> In stature, Boru of Ballinoe did overtop two good-size yeomen, one standing on the shoulders of the other, and was as broad withal as the horn-span of a twain of oxen yoked side by side. These dimensions are closely observed and such as I can vouch for, having been related to me by a close witness of these dread matters, he being Shawn Calan, a turf-cutter of Ballinoe, who was so fortunate as to escape from the roasting-spit itself. Calan, having despaired of his life and a-swoon from the first heat of the cooking fire, when the rig was overturned by a blow of Boru's foot kicking in anger. The ogre had broken one of his smaller teeth biting down on a man who had been roasted in armor, this being done by Boru's cook on his master's command, who fancied it might be like unto boiling a lobster in its shell. However, roaring with pain from his broken tooth, Boru delivered that kick at the spit which was Calan's salvation, for it (the spit) flew out of the roasting pit and was shattered on the flagstones, allowing the half-charred man to crawl away in much agony of body but thankful in his soul, and so he made his escape.

And this was the brute Finn saw charging upon him as he balanced himself on his stilts in the middle of the stream. Topping that enormous body was a face more horrible than any the lad had ever dreamed in his deepest nightmare. A man's face, but resembling that of a giant boar, with long heavy needle-pointed tusks curving from its mouth, and eyes like two drops of blood. Finn, swaying there on his poles in the rushing stream, was completely helpless. He could neither run nor fight.

Boru reached him, seized him by the neck, and lifted him in the air as easily as if he were a kitten. But Finn held onto his stilts, and, dangling there in the monster's hands, he kicked twice, once with his left foot, and once with his right. The left-footed kick sliced off the elbow of Boru's raised arm, forcing him to release his grip. And Finn's right-footed kick drove a hole through the gross bladder that was Boru's stomach. The spear quivered there in the torn belly. Finn released the haft of both spears, fell into the water, and dived deep to escape the gouts of blood spouting from Boru's wound. But he had no sooner surfaced than an enormous weight fell on him—Boru's body it was—driving him to the bottom of the stream before he had time to take breath.

He would have drowned there, perhaps, but the falcon shot into the air, folded her wings and dropped—not like a gull, but like the diving fishhawk who goes deep to find its prey underwater. The falcon grasped Finn's belt and dragged him to the surface, and the lad was able to stumble to shore, choking and gasping.

Boru's body now lay in the stream, which ran red. The giant was big enough to walk on, and this Finn did, walking out and kneeling upon Boru's shoulders, wrenching the huge head around and slicing it off. He held it high, dripping, tusks glittering in the watery light, as he walked back over his foe's body to the shore.

"Truly," he said to the falcon, "you are the very Queen of hawks, and I choose you for an important errand. Take this ugly head by the hair and fly it back to Tara. Upon the tusk I impale this note which says that I, Finn McCool, have accomplished my first task, dispatching the Boar of Ballinoe."

The falcon flew away carrying the head, still dripping blood. And in the tales of those days they speak of a rain of blood that fell strangely upon the southern counties after the Great Frost and the Great Thaw.

Houlihan's Barn

pon the scroll at Tara whereon were listed Finn's tasks was written "Houlihan's Barn." What these words meant he had no idea, nor did he attempt to learn, knowing that it was the nature of such labors to disclose themselves in their own way. But the fact of it is—and a fact or two, but not too many, will fit pleasantly into a true story—the fact of it is that Houlihan's wife, when he had one in the long ago, was altogether too tidy. How Houlihan had come to choose her is a mystery. He was a big brawling red-pelted man; the only time he bathed was when he was caught in the rain. No member of his family had worn shoes since the dawn of time, nor did he ever use knife at table, but tore the meat with his hands, then wiped them on his beard. Yet when it came time to marry, why, he chose this brisk little person who fairly shone with cleanliness, and who shook with fury at the mere shadow of dust. Why did he woo her? Why did she allow herself to be won? There is a puzzle between man and woman

beyond ordinary meaning, and time can turn a girl into a hag and a
man into a stick and the mystery into a gall, but it is born again at
wakes and weddings—which is perhaps why they are so popular.

Anyway, this little wife of Houlihan's took the stinking pigpen
that was his farm and made it sweet as a garden of herbs. By god,
when she was finished the pigs smelled like violets; there was not a
nettle or briar to be seen on the place; her pots hung over the hob
like dark suns, and fence and barn were whitewashed so white it hurt
the eye to look at them. She cleaned up her husband, too. Wouldn't
let him near her on their wedding night, rumor said, until he had
soaked himself in the river for a full hour, scrubbing himself raw
while she stood on the bank telling him what to do. And after she had
him awhile, why, hair and beard were clipped, and he was combed
and curried and scrubbed and rubbed until he was sleek as an otter.
And he seemed happy that way, and anyone who dared jest about new
ways or new wife felt the weight of his fist, which was the heaviest in
that part of Leinster.

But for all her bustle her ways were never grim. Light-footed she
was, and pleasant of voice; built small with sapling grace, she
seemed to distill light as she went. Too much, perhaps. For certain
drees of darkness were deep offended and resolved to blot her. Of
what she most loathed they took the essence and concocted a creature.
Out of rot and stench, slime, dead birds, roaches, rats, they cooked up
something that looked like a huge ball of clotted hair, something between a sow and a spider, but ten feet round. And one day in the early
light as she was weeding her garden it rolled upon her blotting her
light.

Big Red Houlihan was left with a two-month old daughter and
a house and fields shining with memory, and a bewilderment turning
into rage, that turned into pure hell-spite.

He killed one or two of his neighbors in the first days of his

wrath, but simple murder left him unslaked. He needed to go beyond
man in his killing. With mighty blows of his axe he knocked down
his house, and moved into the barn. He could not sleep, so to fill his
nights he went cattle-raiding, hoping to be caught and killed after a
last bloody brawl. But, by prudence or design, his neighbors left him
strictly alone even when he was helping himself to their stock. He
herded the stolen cows and pigs in great droves into his barn. Nor
did he ever clean that barn, but lived there with his little daughter in
the muck and mire which grew more dreadful each day.

Finally Houlihan's barn had become the biggest midden in all
Eire, an unbelievable putrid heap that stank all his neighbors out of
that part of the country and put a taint upon the air clear to Meath.
When the wind was right, it was said, you could smell that barn
across the Giant's Causeway all the way into Scotland. And at the very
center of this mountain of filth lived Houlihan, so foul now he could
scarcely be distinguished from one of his dung-splattered bulls. Here,
too, among the crud-worms and flies the size of sparrows, grew his
daughter; nor could anyone tell what she looked like, so thick was
her mask of dirt.

Now this daughter, whose name was Kathleen, loved her father
because he belonged to her, and was even fond of her home, for she
knew no other. Nevertheless, as she grew older she grew restless, until
one day Houlihan said:

"Now stop your wriggling and squirming, girl. You need a husband to calm you down."

"A husband!" she shrieked. "And who would marry me in my
filthy state?"

"Why, whatever lad I catch for you—after I explain his duties
a time or two."

"Thank you. I'll catch my own."

"Then be about it, and good luck to you. But be sure you bring him here to live, for I need you to serve me, and he can help."

"Bring him back to this muck and mire? Why should I?"

"Because I tell you to."

"Why should he?"

"You will not find me meddling in those delicate questions that arise between man and bride. I am sure you will be able to put the matter to him persuasively, for you were ever a dutiful girl, and it is I who bid you, I, Red Houlihan, who curses every day that keeps him on this pitiful dung heap of an earth, and in the long deep blackness of whose life you have been the only light."

"I'm off," said she. "I'll be back with my husband, or perhaps alone."

"One last word," said Houlihan. "Seek your love on the far bank of a river that has no bridge."

"Yes, father."

Now, on the other side of the river there lived a gentle-mannered smiling sort of lad, with hair like peach floss. Nineteen years old he was, but he had been kept quite childlike by his mother, who was known as the Widow of the Cove. The lad's name was Carth. What he liked to do best in the world was lie on a rock in the sun, thinking nothing at all until pictures began drifting through his head. He did not know where they came from or where they were going, but he liked to watch them while they were there. One day the same picture kept swimming into his head. A girl, dripping wet.

Now, as it happened, in his nineteen years he had never seen a girl of any kind, wet or dry. His mother had kept him from all such, fearing that one of the greedy creatures might decide to marry her boy before he was ripe. And this thought threw her into such a rage that she kept him close to his own homestead, nor allowed him to roam.

So when he saw this wet girl in a waking dream, she made the first he had ever seen, and he doted upon her, saying to himself:

"Oh, how happy I would be if she were real. How softly I would welcome her, offering to do her any service—to chop wood and fetch water, and slop her pigs, and milk her cow, and lay a fire in her hearth so that she might dry herself in its warmth, combing out her long red hair. She must be real, though, must she not, else whence comes this image of her in my head? Could it come of itself? Impossible. It must be some shadow of an actual girl with such length of thigh and flesh of eye and lamb-tongue smoothness of flesh and fiery pennant of hair—for I have no power of invention to so paint her for myself. Nor is it memory, for I have never seen the like or near it, nor any woman indeed but my own mother whose dear skin is like a prune and hair like wire. She must be real then, and being real must be somewhere near, else why should her shadow tease and tangle me so?"

When he opened his eyes he saw a wet girl on the riverbank wringing out her long wet hair, and he did not know whether the dream had made her come or she had made the dream come, and he didn't care.

"Good morning to you," he said. "I am Carth of the Cove."

"And good morning to you, sweet lad. Kathleen is my name. My father is Houlihan, of whom you may have heard."

"Not I. I have heard of nothing, and seen less. My mother keeps me close."

"Mother? Are you not too big now to be having a mother?"

"It would seem not. I certainly have one. And she has me. She is a widow, you see, and childless save for me."

"What do you know of kissing and such?"

"Oh, she kisses me good night every night. And upon my birthday, you know. A dry flinching sort of business. Don't think much of it."

"Have you never been properly kissed by a girl?"

"You are the first girl I have ever met up close."

"Well, you have lots to learn and I have lots to teach, only I shall have to learn too while teaching—so let's be about it."

"Do you mean to commence now?"

"Now. Certainly now. In these matters it is always now. In fact, as I see you sitting up there sweet and savory as a roast piglet, I understand that this all should have happened before. I am fair famished for you, little pig."

"But my mother has warned me about girls. I must not meet them, nor meeting, look, nor looking, speak, nor speaking, touch. I'm to avoid them altogether, the lovely fresh rain-smelling creatures. She will not have me marry until I am forty."

"Will she not?"

"She is most resolute. Promises to flay the skin off my backside if I do not heed her."

"And I promise worse if you do."

Some days later Finn was walking along a riverbank in Leinster, harp slung, attended by cat and falcon, when a voice shrieked:

"Halt!"

It was a woman standing on the road with wild hair and flying shawls, face lumpy and red as a fist. Finn stopped at her word.

"Good day, mistress. May I serve you?"

"Have you seen a boy on your travels?"

"One or two. What class of boy would you be seeking?"

"An imbecile."

"I have met such, indeed. What does your imbecile look like?"

"Sweet, sweet, with angel-blue eyes and peach-bloom cheek. Soft-spoken, gentle, all dewy with a mother's kisses."

"I do not believe I have met this lad. But I can understand how you grieve to lose such a son."

"Lose him . . . lose him . . . I never did. He was stolen."

"By whom?"

"I'm not sure. But my mother's intuition tells me it was a girl, who came by water, the slut, to avoid my vigil. Came secretly, leering and fleering, to carry the lamb off to her bed."

And the woman danced in her rage, singing:

> Calamity, disaster,
> Pestilence and plague.
> I'll scarify and blast her,
> break her head like an egg.

Then she turned to Finn, and said:

"You are a doer of deeds, are you not, young sir?"

"I am, lady. Certain tasks claim my attention."

"And you are sworn to aid the weak and helpless, are you not?"

"I am."

"Then you must help me."

"Would you be describing yourself as weak and helpless?"

"Damn your eyes if I am not! I am a poor lorn widow who has been cheated out of her only son by some sly vixen whom I will strangle with these two hands when I find her. You will help me, will you not?"

"In my opinion, widow, it is your enemies who will be needing help."

"Oh woe and wail-away, how can I find them. They are fleet and I am slow. If I do not appeal to your chivalry, let me try your greed. For thirty years have I been skimping and scrimping and now I have a pot of gold. A double handful of the lovely stuff do I offer if you help me find my boy."

"Keep your gold, lady. My deeds are not for sale. Nor am I free to refuse you aid however I may sympathize with your son and his abductress. I will help you find them. But once found, what follows is up to you. I will not meddle more."

"Just locate my Carth for me and I will do the rest, and be grateful to you forever."

"Farewell, madame."

Not long after this the widow received a note from her son that read:

Dear Mother:

You're wondering what happened to me. Well, it seems that I'm married now to this girl who swam the river that morning and told me what I had to do to be her husband. I told her you didn't mean me to get married until I was forty, but she wouldn't listen. At first we were going to live in her father's barn, but after a few nights she decided that I wouldn't last long if she took me home because he's very large and fierce, and gets angry quite easily and has other peculiar ways. So we have set up housekeeping in a very comfortable hollow tree with a view of the river. Being a husband is pretty strange. You have to do all sorts of things you never did before. But it's enjoyable, too, in its own way most of the time, and I'm doing quite well for a beginner, my wife says. Her name is Kathleen. Please come and visit us and stay as long as you like. Kathleen joins me in this invitation. She says no matter how bad you are her father is worse, and living with him has taught her to fear neither man, beast, nor devil. Indeed it is true, she is very brave.

Love,
Carth.

You can imagine how angry the widow was when she read this letter. She fumed and raged and stamped her foot and clawed the air and smashed a whole roomful of furniture before the red mist of her tantrum cleared and a little sense came back. She seized the note and went rampaging down the road until she found Finn's encampment.

"Good morning, widow," he said. "I did not expect to see you again so soon."

"Nor I you," said the widow. "Look at this."

She thrust the note at him. He read it and smiled.

"Well," he said. "This seems to let me off the hook."

"What hook? What hook? What do you mean off?"

"I mean I am no longer bound to find them. They have found themselves and told you where they are."

"You still must help me," she cried. "Don't you see this is a trap? She forced him to write this weasel-worded invitation. He never did it himself, poor stupid intimidated darling. She made him write it, threatening some awful torment to his tender flesh. Now she awaits my coming with a meat cleaver up her sleeve and kettles full of poison brewing on the stove in case she gets to serve me tea. You must come with me and protect me against assassination like the young hero you are.

"Perhaps if you speak gently to your son's wife, and do not accuse her of kidnapping the lad by force, and try to treat her as a human being instead of some wild beast—why, then, perhaps, she in turn will hang up her meat cleaver and save her vial of poison for another occasion. And you two will sit and drink tea and converse like two civilized creatures. Is that not possible?"

"Drink tea with that murdering slut, is it, in her hollow-tree den? Give myself into her treacherous hands completely? And never see light of day again? Is that what you propose? No, my fine Finn, you must keep your hero vows and come with me, and help me thwart the plans of that red-headed young assassin, who has stolen away the innocent son, and now wishes to rid herself of the poor grievin' mother."

"Well, there's no hope for it," said Finn. "I see that I must accompany you on this charming visit. But I am not free until the day after the day after tomorrow."

"So be it," said the Widow. "In two days' time you and I will go together to visit Kathleen ni Houlihan, and see what is to be done to save my boy."

But it was not yet to be. On the evening of that day a mighty storm struck the coast, one of the worst in memory, sending huge seas to drown the beaches, tossing boulders like pebbles, leveling whole forests.

Finn was comfortable enough in his cave, and did not wholly regret the storm. "For," he thought to himself, "it may be that the hollow tree where dwelt the troublesome bride and groom has fallen in the storm like so many trees, and they forced to search for another dwelling where the widow cannot find them. As for that harridan, who knows? Perhaps she was swept out to sea by a wave, or caught in the open by a wind and blown quite out of my life. Well, we'll just wait and see."

After the storm Finn was left alone. His companions, the cat and the hawk, had departed gleefully—for hunting is good in the aftermath of a storm. And the next day the widow appeared.

"Stir your stumps in there!" she called. "Today is the day you keep your promise, Finn. We go a-visiting, you and I."

So it was that Finn on that fair, cold, blue-and-gold, after-the-storm morning found himself in the middle of a dreadful scene. For the raging widow hunted down the young couple. The hollow tree was gone. The forest itself was a tangled thicket of fallen timber where the great trees had been scythed down by the wind. But the woman let nothing discourage her. She followed her nose like a bloodhound, and led Finn straight to the banks of a river where stood the hull of a wrecked ship. Here Kathleen and her spouse had set up housekeeping.

There was no exchange of greetings. The widow let out a bloody howl and leaped right onto the ribbed hull of the ship, cocking her blackthorn cane to knock Kathleen's head off her shoulders. But the girl never flinched. Swift as a snake striking, she reached her long arm and twisted the stick out of the widow's clutch and broke it over her knee, then strode to the widow and stood facing her.

"Is this how you come a-calling, Mother dear? Were you never in all your long years taught manners, by any chance? Well, you've come to the right place to learn."

Finn and Carth stood horror-struck, watching the women. Mother and wife stood crouched, eye to eye, nose to nose, jawbone to jawbone, too close to shriek, but berating each other in strangled whispers.

"He's mine, mine, mine, and you shan't have him!"

"He's mine now, and I shall keep him!"

"He has me, and needs no other!"

"He needs me, not his mother!"

Now the widow wound her claws into Kathleen's red hair and tried to pull it out by the roots. But the girl braced herself like a powerful white mare, stiffened the column of her neck, then snapped her head, and the long red pelt of her hair snapped like a whip, snapping the widow off her feet and hurling her the length of the deck, where she fetched up against a rusty anchor. She rushed upon Kathleen, screaming:

"I'll tear the blue eyes out of your head, you wild hussy!"

"Come and try, Mother dear," crooned Kathleen, crouching, and rocking her long arms.

Now Carth of the Cove, who could not bear to see them fight like this, the two women in his life, rushed between them—unwisely, for each seized an arm and a leg, and pulled at him, crying:

"He's mine, he's mine, he's mine!"

"Drop this wife, and come away with me, dearie," cried his mother, pulling with all her might.

"Cast off this mother and stay with me," said Kathleen, pulling with all her wondrous might.

Flesh and bone could not take this tugging. The boy came apart in their hands. Split right in two, he did, from crotch to pate. The mother was left holding half a son by arm and leg—one arm, one leg, one haunch, one shoulder, half a face split right up the bridge of the nose. And Kathleen, for her part, held half a husband, precisely the other half—and each half useless to mother and wife.

Finn, in a rage, leaped across the deck, and seized the halves of the boy from the women's hands, and laid them tenderly down— then clouted each warring woman along the side of the jaw, laying them out flat.

"Sure," he said, "you two are the shrews of the world and impossible for a man to deal with. Now look what you've done to this poor lad. Aye, and it shall be long work knitting him together, if indeed it can be done at all. For it takes much magic to restore a lad so split and torn."

He found a hole of the right size where a small tree had been uprooted and stuck the widow in headfirst. It was a bit narrow, but he jammed her in till she fit snug, with only her feet sticking in the air.

"She's too tough to kill and too mean to die," said Finn to himself, "but this will cool her off a bit."

There she had to stay, upside down in her hole, where she could howl and gnash her teeth and disturb nothing but the worms, who are unsympathetic. And her shrieks would come out muffled as the pleasant little creakings of earth you hear among the grass sometimes in summer; and the bitter tears of her wrath would lose their bile and bubble to earth, unembittered, as fresh springs.

He began to look for another hole for Kathleen. But then he remembered suddenly the blue flame of her eyes, and the limber column of her neck, and her hair red as the oak leaf in autumn. And he returned to her and lifted her out of the wrecked ship and took her to the river, where he laved her face until the cool water awakened her. She looked at him silently.

He said: "On second thought you shall journey with me, to the far home of Angus Og whose magic I will implore to rejoin the halves of your poor husband, whom you and your mother-in-law between you have succeeded in tearing apart. For it is a far journey I make and a great boon I ask at the end of it, and a heavyweight of dead body I carry in this sack—so I shall not leave you here, but you will come with me and help. It is your husband in the sack, after all."

"Who are you?" said Kathleen. "And why do you thrust yourself into my household affairs?"

"I am Finn McCool. And I advise you to ask no more questions in that tone, my girl, or I may clout you on the other side of the jaw. For you are a beautiful creature to look at, but a terrible shrew. As for your household affairs, I wish I were heartily out of them. But I am under hero vow to do favors when asked, and I was asked. And here I am. So shut you up, and come along."

That night, after their evening meal, as they sat on a bluff overlooking the sea upon which a roadway had been kindled by the moon, there was a rustling in the air, and a flash of green fire from four wild eyes, high and low, and Finn's companions, the hawk and the cat, came to him from where they had been off hunting.

The falcon perched on Finn's shoulder. The cat, without hesitation, stepped into Kathleen's lap. And Finn noticed with admiration that the girl was not at all frightened by the sudden apparition of a huge black tomcat with blazing green eyes who shot out of the darkness at her. She stroked the cat, saying:

"Good evening to you, Master Puss. You're a handsome beast, to be sure, but I see no one has taught you manners, leaping out of the black darkness like that."

She stroked his head and shoulders, and he closed his eyes and purred his low rasping purr. The falcon said to Finn:

"I have a tale for your ears. May I tell it now?"

"Tell away," said Finn.

"Lord McCool, tell me—did I hear that bird speak to you, and you answering it?" said Kathleen.

"You did."

"Well, that's a marvel now," said the girl.

"Not so marvelous," said the cat. "I speak too. And in more cultivated tones—without that screeching hawky accent."

" You too!" cried Kathleen. "Well, I have been turned out of my peaceable home, and seem to find myself in the middle of an adventure, with strange companions. A meddlesome gray-eyed stripling who calls himself hero, and minds everyone's business for them, and claims an acquaintanceship with sorcerers, and a hawk that speaks, and a cat who boasts of even greater eloquence. Sure, and I've fallen into curious company."

"You've known worse," said Finn.

"May I tell you my story," said the falcon. "I seem to have been interrupted."

"Proceed," said Finn.

"It's the kind of thing that interests you, master. An adventure within an adventure, as it were. And all of it holding enough peril to suit even you."

"I'm listening," said Finn.

"I heard this story from a gull—with whom I had been disputing property rights over the carcass of a fat fish, which he had caught, to be sure, but which I had made him drop. Anyway, he was a pleasant enough bird for a gull; we resolved our quarrel and got to chatting of this and that. And he told me there was soon going to be a terrible fish shortage because of the anger of Lyr, God of the Sea.

" 'Why is he angry?' I asked.

'You would be angry too, if you were a prisoner.'

'Lyr, a prisoner? But who can imprison a god?'

'Another god, of course,' said the gull. 'Here's what happened. Some months ago Lyr was on one of his rare trips inland to inspect certain rivers which flow to the sea, and which are part of his domain. He spied a beautiful ice maiden, dispatched by Vilemurk, god of winter, to delay the spring and blow her sweet icy breath upon various streams and ponds that were trying to thaw, and freeze them fast, though the month was April. Lyr watched the ice maiden for a while, and liked what he saw. He flung his green cape about her and flew back with her to his crystal and coral island in the very middle of the seven seas. She resisted at first, but he promised her this and that, if she would consent to stay with him and become his youngest wife. It meant being a queen, of course, and he promised her the choicest pearls of the oyster crop, and an ivory comb curiously carved, and her own dolphin chariot, and a mermaid's tail and gills for when she wished to travel underwater. And so she agreed to stay with him and become the most recent and most beautiful of all his briny brides.'

"All this the gull told me, master. And I listened patiently, though it is not my nature. For I could see that there was trouble coming in the story, and that's worth waiting for."

"Get to the trouble, then," said Finn.

"Yes, it came immediately," said the hawk.

And she went on with the story the gull had told her, and which goes like this: Now, Vilemurk, whom some call the frost demon, was hugely angry when he learned that someone had stolen his favorite ice maiden, and that this someone was his old enemy, Lyr, whom he had always hated because huff and puff and chill as he would, he could never freeze the wide seas. All except that one time, remember, in the year of the Great Frost, when Finn first started on his journeys, and took the seeds of fire from the frozen sunset. But even then the sea was frozen for only a short distance past its shores. And so, Vilemurk, King of Winter, had always hated Lyr, God of the Sea. And now, of course, he hated him worse than ever, with a hatred that had to end in death or torment.

What he did then was spread a tale of a treasure in the northern seas where Vilemurk holds more power than other places, and keeps great fleets of ice thronging the open waters, and has dyed all the animals the color of snow. Well, the rumor he spread was one meant to appeal to Lyr, lover of all that glitters. A giant crystal, the rumor said, had been spotted floating on the black northern waters. A pure water crystal larger than the largest iceberg, hard as a diamond, and so carved by aeons of knife-edged polar winds that it was all polished surfaces and glittering angles. When the sun hit it, the giant crystal blazed forth with rainbow light, making all the jewels of earth seem drabber than the pebbles you find in the dust.

Rumor of this wondrous crystal fired Lyr with a wild greed. And he rushed off north to see for himself. Left in such haste that he left behind his escort of swordfish and spearfish and fire-eels and shark-toothed mermen, and all-ignorant and unguarded sped northward to where his enemy, Vilemurk, lay in ambush.

Now Vilemurk had brought with him all the disastrous giants that the foul-weather fiend commanded:

The huge coiled serpentine monster that lies underearth, stone asleep, until he awakes in rage to make earth quake.

And the giants who dwell in hollow mountains whose cooking fires are called volcanoes.

And the Master of Winds, who can whistle up a hurricane as a man whistles for his dog.

All these and more: The bat-winged mist-hags, who, flying low and in formation, can lay a blindness upon earth and sea. Those same chill crones whose fingers are icicles and whose breath can freeze the marrow. When they have nothing else to do they go about robbing the cradles of girl-babies and train them up as ice maidens.

All these lay in wait for the god of the sea. Lyr came northward, traveling alone in his sky chariot drawn by flying fishes. Toward a rumored treasure and an unknown foe he rushed, standing tall in his chariot, clad in whaleskin armor with a mantle of seal furs swinging from his mighty shoulders; wearing his crown of pearls, white beard flying, holding his three-pronged spear, which he could hurl like a thunderbolt if he wished, or handle as delicately as a seamstress does her needle. Northward he came, flashing across the low horizon, making a strange sun in the northern sky, which was entering its season of night.

All a-glitter, hot with greed, Lyr came riding across the sky to seek the huge gem of water crystal he had heard about—and flew right into Vilemurk's ambush.

Such was the tale the hawk told Finn, sitting on his shoulder in a clearing of the wood where the little fire Kathleen had cooked supper on made tree shadows dance. But Finn and the tall girl sat motionless among the dancing shadows, still and rapt, drinking in the words of the strange tale told by the hawk, who had heard it from a gull.

"Go on!" said Finn. "Don't stop now, just when Lyr is about to be trapped."

"Flying *fish*," hissed the falcon. "Imagine fish flying. Disgusting! Sure, and Lyr deserved what happened to him, employing such unnatural creatures."

The cat yawned in the firelight, half turning on Kathleen's lap, and lifted a paw to play with a plume of her hair.

"But what *did* happen to Lyr?" crooned Kathleen. "Don't leave us hangin', falcon dear. 'Tis a fearsome exciting tale, and you tell it so well. Did he fall into Vilemurk's trap, or what? Was he ambushed there by the frost demon in the northern wastes? Was there a battle perhaps? Tell . . . tell. . . ."

"Remember the big storm a few days back?" said the hawk.

"Oh, yes," said Kathleen. "It fair leveled the forest over our heads. And didn't mighty waves pound the beaches, swallowing up fishing huts, sweeping away barns and byres, drowning cattle. Most terrible storm in years it was—and the next day my mother-in-law came a-callin'."

"Well, that terrible storm, Kathleen ni Houlihan, was only a tiny ripple of the tempest that raged in the north when the forces of Vilemurk came screaming out of ambush and fell upon the sea king."

"Go on . . . what happened?"

"I don't mean to leave you in suspense," said the hawk. "But, unfortunately, I cannot finish the story . . . because the gull never finished it. He got too hungry. The fish had been very scarce, and when he saw the shadow of a trout he dived at it, leaving me there. I waited for him, but he never came back. So he must have kept on hunting, and I don't know how the battle ended."

No one said anything. Kathleen stared into the fire. The flames snapped. The cat yawned. Suddenly, across the orange face of the moon were pasted the black silhouettes of wild geese. A long flight of them, necks outthrust, wings low, honking faintly, almost a barking sound, like hounds of the sky.

The hawk rose in the air and balanced herself just above Finn's head.

"Good night, master!" she cried. "I go a-hunting. We eat goose tomorrow."

She disappeared. The honking grew clamorous, alarmed—then nothing was heard save the snapping of the fire.

"What do you think, lad?" said Kathleen. "What happened out there in the northern wastes? How went the battle? Did Vilemurk conquer Lyr? Did Lyr prevail? Tell me your opinion."

Finn said nothing, but stared into the fire, gently biting his thumb.

"Don't sit there sucking at your thumb like an idiot child," cried Kathleen. "I asked you a question. I want an answer. I get excited by stories. I don't like them to stop before they end. And a good guess is better than nothing."

"You have no way of knowing," said Finn. "But I'll tell you now. I don't have to guess, because when I bite my thumb this way, the very one that was scorched when I fried the fish of knowledge—which is another story I may tell you sometime—why then knowledge comes to me, and I know beyond guessing. I invoke this power only upon special occasions. Not for little secrets, you understand. But the fate of the sea god seems occasion enough. And, as I bite my thumb this way, pictures appear in the fire, and I can see them."

"What do you see?" said Kathleen. "Tell me . . . tell me . . . ."

"I see right into the awful depths of the earth that opens out under the sea, void under void. I see beyond those depths into the central fires of the earth, whence grows a pillar of rock, molten rock far under, then cooling, cooling, until finally cooled by the northern sea, where the rock turns into ice. From this granite base grows a mountain of ice, which is like a huge iceberg, but does not float. And beneath this mountain, right where the granite turns into ice, there to that massive shaft is chained Lyr—shackled by the heaviest bolts ever made by those smith-gods who labor inside Vilemurk's smoky mountains and forge his weapons in the volcano fires."

"You see all that?" whispered Kathleen.

"Indeed I do."

"What else do you see?"

"Tilted in the flame I see the oceans of the world. They are lead-colored now, and have lost their shine. No fish leap, no gulls fly. Crabs and lobsters crawl out of the seven surfs, fleeing the beaches, and trying to climb trees. Yes, there is grief upon the waters, for the god has fallen."

"Is he dead?"

"Gods cannot die. But they can suffer. And this one is suffering. Chained underearth, deprived of water and light and majesty—tormented by Vilemurk's bat-winged mist-hags who gnaw at him with their snaggly teeth—aye, he suffers. And the waters grieve. And those who live off the bounty of the sea, sailors and fishermen and such, they will perish, too."

"Terrible pictures you see there in the fire," said Kathleen.

"Yes . . . and I go to change them."

"What?"

"I go to free the god of the sea."

"You? What can you do?"

"That is what I mean to find out. Farewell. I go north."

"And what am I to do, young sir, while you go cavorting off on your adventures? What am I to do with that bag of bones that was my husband? It is your fault I am in such a plight. If you had not brought his mother to see me, I'd still be living happily with him in my hollow tree. But no! You must try to act like a hero and meddle in my affairs, and bring that old witch raging down upon us, so that the poor lad was torn apart."

"But I have promised to restore him," said Finn. "I deny that he was sundered by my doing; nevertheless, I have taken it upon myself to see him whole again. It is only by the mighty magic of Angus Og that his poor bones can be reknitted."

"Exactly," said Kathleen. "And you are supposed to be taking us to Angus Og. But now you abandon us. You choose to go waltzing off on some conceited errand to the northern wastes. I'll not have it! You must keep your promise to me, and leave the god of the sea to those better able to conduct such high affairs."

"Will you be silent, woman?" cried Finn. "Buzz, buzz, buzz—I cannot think! Nag, nag, nag—you drive me to distraction! Can't you see that I have no choice, despite my promise? I am shown a larger danger, and I must choose it. To challenge Vilemurk and rescue Lyr is a deed worthy of Cuchulain himself, best of the ancient heroes. It puts me in a fever to think of such opportunity. So you must wait. Your husband must wait. My promise must wait."

"Wait how long?"

"Till I return."

"And if you fail to return? If Vilemurk is powerful enough to capture the king of the sea himself, what makes you think, puny mortal that you are, that he will not squash you like a bug?"

"Without peril there is no honor."

"And so—you will be destroyed. And I will wait here with my sack of bones through the long years until I grow old and gray and withered and wouldn't know what to do with a husband if I had one. No, thank you. I am your responsibility now. You thrust yourself into my business and made it yours. I am not so easy to get rid of, you will find. Go north if you must, but I go with you."

"Kathleen—be reasonable. I have fighting to do. I'll have no time to take care of you."

"Perhaps I'll take care of you. I can fight too, you know. And pretty well . . . pretty well. So you may as well stop arguing. You won't budge me. Where you go, I go, and that's flat. As for this bag of bones that is my husband—well, we'll store it in a safe place, and pick it up when we return, if we return. There's a good flat rock. We'll bury the bones under it, and they'll be safe from prowling dogs.

Start digging, Finn. The moon grows pale, and the waters grieve, and we have much to do, you and I."

Vilemurk had conquered, and his forces were everywhere at work, shrinking the seas, stretching the polar ice cap. The north wind blew triumphantly, sweeping the warm sea southward, and paving the path of its retreat with rock-hard ice tundra.

Vanquished Lyr, manacled hand and foot to the granite pillar of ice that supported the roof of the world, could not struggle free. His oceans shrank, and fishermen and sailors perished.

It was only autumn, but the coldest autumn Ireland had ever known. Ice-cold rain fell without ceasing. The sun was all shriveled to a pinpoint of light, when it could be seen at all, but mostly it was not seen, for a queer cold fog covered the shores, confusing day and night. As the month advanced, the cold rain turned to hailstones big as eggs that fell with such force as to kill cattle in the field. Men did not venture out unless they wore helmets. Their wives, when they left the house, wore iron pots on their heads. Then, before October ended, the snow began to sift down out of the gray sky. And fell and fell and fell. No one knew what had happened to the weather, and why the frost demon triumphed so, and was able to torment those islands known as the jewels of the sea.

Of all men, only Finn knew, he and Kathleen. And they were far to the north, fighting through a howling blizzard on their way to try to rescue Lyr. They were clad in white fur, which made them very difficult to see against the snow. Finn had gone hunting and had come back with a pair of huge polar-bear pelts, which Kathleen had cut and sewed into two mantles and two hoods for herself and Finn. These furs kept them warm in the teeth of the savage north wind.

That night they held a council of war around their campfire.

And how did they build a fire in a blizzard with no tree in sight, and no earth beneath their feet, only ice? Well, you will remember the seeds of fire that Finn, once, in another great frost, had dug from the roots of a frozen sunset before its weight tilted the horizon and it slipped toward the pole and lodged in that sky, casting marvelous colors, and became known as the Northern Lights. Finn had kept these seeds of fire always. Now, each night, he scraped a shaving off one of the pulsing golden pods, and that shaving was enough to start a fire anywhere—for it was a particle of the primal flame itself, that heat which is at the center of all life and drops to us from the sun. Each night Finn started a small blaze which he fed with icicles, and the flame ate them as if they were twigs of wood, and leaped merrily, hissing and growing brighter as the snow fell upon it.

How did Finn carry these seeds of fire, then, without getting holes burned right through him? Well, when he dug out the seeds he went to a secret underground workshop where labor the craftsmen of the Tuatha da Danaan, those ancient gods of Ireland who have shrunk up because people ceased believing in them, but who can still do magic when necessary. They work underground, polishing gems, tanning leather for the finest boots, making daggers for kings and such. The chief tanner there became interested in Finn's problem when it was explained to him, and fabricated a very special leather to make a pouch for the seeds of fire. The problem was to make it cold enough; to do that was needed the coldest hides in all the world. Now the cruelest and coldest of all the animals is man at his worst, and the coldest part of him is his heart. So, from a storage bin the tanner drew out the heart of a miser and the heart of a tyrant and the wizened heart of a bard whom no one listened to, spun a thread of tiger sinew, mixed a paste of shark's blood and snake spit and crocodile tears, and sewed Finn a pouch, speckled, greenish-brown, beautiful—and demonishly cold. So cold it could hold the seeds of fire, and Finn could carry them at his belt without harm.

Finn had told this story to Kathleen over the first campfire made from the fire seed, and it was a wonder to the girl. She loved handling the pouch and watching the seed sprout its magic flame. They sat about their fire on this night then and plotted what to do. The hawk perched on Finn's shoulder and the huge black tomcat lay in Kathleen's lap. And their fire was the only spot of light in all that howling waste.

"We've almost come to where I want to go," said Finn. "But what to do when we get there I do not know."

"That sounds like a song," said Kathleen. "A sad song."

"Yes, and I beg your pardon. A true hero should grow more joyous as his hour of peril approaches. But I am no true hero, you know."

"I didn't know. How could I tell? You're the only one I've met, true or untrue."

"Well, take my word for it. By nature I'm a coward. I just pretend to be brave. And sometimes the pretense wears thin. I hate fighting. I can't bear the sight of blood. I don't even like loud noises."

"What in the world are we doing here then, picking a quarrel with the frost demon himself and all his fearsome friends? Why must you pretend to be brave if you're not?"

"It's a funny thing about courage. If you pretend hard enough it becomes real."

"Ridiculous! Why should you have to be a hero in the first place?"

"I didn't have much choice," said Finn gloomily. "My father was a hero. And various uncles. And grandfathers and great-grandfathers by the bushel, stretching back to the original family of giants who bullied their way onto this island and chased smaller folk off. I was the runt of the litter. Everyone was disappointed in me, and no one expected much in the way of sword play and such. But, as it happened, I was even more contrary than I was cowardly. I decided to change myself, and went to work becoming what everyone expected me not to be. I have sought dreadful adventures, and have come through with honor. But before every battle, I'm afraid. I'm afraid right now. But maybe I'll forget about it when the fighting starts."

"Are we close to fighting then?"

"Close enough. See that giant pile of ice glimmering off yonder? That's the end of our journey. In the side of that ice mountain is the mouth of a cave. The cave winds down to the base of the mountain, which is the granite shaft to which Lyr is chained. The mouth of that cave is the doorway to our adventure."

"So you mean to go down there and rescue him? Is that it?" said Kathleen.

"Ah, I wish it were as easily done as said. You see, I haven't told you about the dragon."

"What dragon?"

"The one that stands guard over Lyr."

"There's a dragon down there?"

"There is."

"That's all that's needed to make a bad case worse."

"Yes. . . ."

"Actually, I don't really know what a dragon is. I've heard about them in the old tales, but I've never seen one."

"Well, those who have don't usually last long enough to tell about it."

"Are they that bad?"

"Worse. Imagine a lizard. . . . You've seen a lizard, haven't you?"

"Yes . . . nasty scuttling little reptiles with long tongues like springs that uncoil to catch bugs on the wing."

"Well, imagine a lizard grown as large as a barn, with teeth the size of plowshares, sharp as knives. And great leathery wings to fly with. All of him covered with leather scales so thick and tough he cannot be wounded by sword or spear wielded by the mightiest warrior. Now this creature has a tail half the length of his body. This tail, when he lashes it, becomes an enormous flail. He can knock over houses with it. Wreck ships. Beat a whole team of oxen flat, and smash the wagon. Yes, a dragon's tail is the most fearsome weapon in all nature. And that's not all. Eight legs the beast has, each of them armed with a set of ripping talons. With a single swipe of his paw he can shred an oak tree."

"Any other features a girl should know about?"

"One more. And that, perhaps, the worst. His breath. It is cold, deathly cold, colder than the essence of frost. When he breathes upon a living creature, its marrow freezes. It turns to ice. This particular dragon has been seen hunting walruses. He breathes their way and petrifies them at the distance of half a mile. Turns them into blocks of ice, and then ambles up to them, and gobbles them down. That's the creature, my dear, who is guarding Lyr down in the cave."

"And you think to go down there and trick the dragon in some way and strike the manacles off the sea god? All by your little self? Confess, isn't that your clever plan?"

"I'm not exactly by myself," said Finn. "I have you, and you have been explaining to me for a thousand miles how formidable you are when aroused. And I have my two trusted friends, the hawk and cat. I have the sword given me by my father and the mission given me by fate."

"I still say it's a mismatch," said Kathleen.

"When mismatched," said Finn, "and that's the case usually with me, for I have not yet reached my full growth, as you know—well, when facing up to a foe overwhelmingly strong, then, I've learned, you must use his own strength against him. That's the secret of winning against odds."

"What exactly do you propose?"

"I don't know exactly. That's why I'm discussing it with you. I'll tell you what there is of my plan, and invite your opinion."

"Thank you."

"Now it is clear that we alone cannot possibly vanquish the frost demon. No . . . it takes a god to conquer another god. Therefore, what we must do is release Lyr so that he may use his power against Vilemurk."

"Release Lyr, is it. That's what I said you were after. I knew that before you started this heavy discussion. But how do you propose to do it?"

"We know that he is manacled to the massive pillar under-earth, and that he is to be reached by entering the cave whose mouth opens out in the slope of that ice mountain yonder. We know also that he is guarded by a dragon."

"It is that dragon who gives me such a poor opinion of our chances," said Kathleen. "You must admit you have painted a fearsome picture of the beast. All he has to do is breathe on us, and there we are, ice statues standing in a cave forever. And that's the best that can happen to us."

"We face a battle," said Finn. "And we have to know the worst so that we can do our best."

"I haven't had an easy life," said Kathleen. "But this worst is worse than any worst I've ever known."

"Well, now, the question is what do we do?" said Finn.

" 'Tis the question indeed. I'm all agog waiting for your an-swer."

"We have discussed the dragon's powers, now we must think about his appetites, for therein may lie a weakness. For instance, what does he eat—besides walruses, which are not his favorite food."

"I can just imagine," said Kathleen, shuddering. "He counts as delicacies, no doubt, lad and lass, and cat and hawk."

"No doubt. But we'd make only a mouthful for him. He needs a more substantial dish, that one. He eats seals by the hundred. Hunts whale and octopus and giant turtle. As for land creatures, he prefers oxen, and such huge viands. Here in the icy waves where game is hard to come by, his favorite meat is polar bear."

"Does he find them way down there at the bottom of the cave?" said Kathleen.

"No," said Finn. "And you have put your finger on the very thing that may give us our chance. To hunt his food he must leave off guarding Lyr and climb to the mouth of the cave, and out upon the ice. There he lies in wait until he spots a polar bear, or a pair of them, and then he dines."

"Stop right there!" said Kathleen.

"What?"

"I'm beginning to get a glimmer of your idea, and I don't like it a bit."

"What don't you like?"

"What you're thinking."

"What am I thinking?"

"That you and I in our polar-bear cloaks and polar-bear hoods —why we look like the dragon's favorite dish ourselves. Isn't that what you're thinking?"

"You're a clever girl."

"Not for long. Soon I'll be a dead girl if I don't look out. Dead and devoured and digested. Oh, why didn't I stay in my father's midden? Why did I have to leave the safety of that stinking pigpen and go husband-hunting across the river? Now look at me—a thousand miles from home and freezing cold and widowed almost before I was wed, and about to become dragon fodder. Oh, woe and wail-away!"

"Have you done with your lamenting?"

"Only for the moment."

"Well, do you want to hear the rest of my plan?"

"Might as well. Don't have anything better to do, and soon things will be much worse."

"Listen, then. In a few hours the dragon will get hungry. He will climb up out of his hole, up through the mountain, out the mouth of the cave, and onto the ice. And what will he see? Well, he will see two polar bears asleep. That's what he'll think he sees, for it is dark, and dragons are nearsighted anyway. So he'll come toward these two sleeping polar bears, who will be us, of course—and we will be waiting for him."

"Without any eagerness whatever," said Kathleen. "Speaking for myself, that is."

"All right . . . he'll come up to the first one, who will be me, and open his great jaws, and prepare to dine."

"Must you go into all this horrible detail," cried Kathleen. "I get the picture."

"Not yet you don't. Look at this."

With a swift movement Finn shed his white cloak and hood, and stood in a black sealskin cape and cap. Kathleen could see only the glitter of his eyes and the shine of his smile. When he tossed his mantle on the ice, why it lay there plumply, looking for all the world like a polar bear.

"I've stuffed it with feathers," said Finn, "which the hawk has been collecting from every bird she strikes down, and which I have been saving for this purpose. Look . . . does it not seem like a polar bear asleep?"

"Yes, it does. And that's about all I can say for it."

"That hide will hold not only feathers," said Finn. "When I finally doff it, it will hold something else, which the dragon will swallow down when he devours this counterfeit bear. And that something else will be this."

He whipped something from his belt and held it toward Kathleen. She peered at it in the firelight.

"Your magic pouch—bearing the seeds of fire!" she cried.

"Exactly. That is what the dragon will swallow. And, perhaps, it will give him the biggest bellyache since bellies were made."

"What about that second sleeping polar bear?" said Kathleen. "The one who's me? Or am I stuffed with feathers and fire too, and hiding in the shadows in a sealskin cape—which, by the way, you haven't given me."

"No," said Finn. "It will be you crouching on the ice in your white cloak. And I have a special task for you. For the dragon will never reach you, if my plan works at all. Once he swallows the seeds of fire he should be very busy for a while. And I will deal with him, and try to control his wrath for our own purpose. And you, you will slip into the mouth of the cave and descend to the depths of the cavern, taking my sword with you. There, you will strike a blow for the shining waters of the world. You will raise my sword, which has been magically honed and can cut through any manacle—you shall wield my sword, you yourself, Kathleen ni Houlihan, too long a daughter, too soon a widow, you Kathleen, beautiful girl, brave and lovely one, who has chosen to leave the bag of bones that was her husband, and come adventuring with Finn McCool into this dire peril. Yes, you will use the sword which passed to me from my father, the great Cuhal, and you will strike the manacles off the god of the sea, and release him to resume the war against the foul-weather fiend and all his cohorts, who hold the seas in bondage and shrink the sun, and starve our folk. You will do this as I do that. Between us, if fortune smiles, and we do not blacken her smile with our own fears, between us we shall conquer."

Kathleen stood tall. There was a deep throb in her voice as she said:

"By the high gods, you can charm the birds off a tree and a girl out of her judgment. I don't know if I'm brave or foolish, but I'm with you till the death."

"What do I do?" said the hawk.

"I have a task for you. You must fly high and strike well to deal with the winged mist-crones who will try to spread a fog about us to bewilder our enterprise."

"And I?" said the cat.

"You will accompany Kathleen to the bottom of the cave, attending every step of her descent. You will need all your wits and claws and all the sorcerous tricks you learned from the Fish-hag to fight off the legions of frost demons that dwell in the cave and make a ferocious horde with their white leather wings and icicle teeth. Task enough for any tom."

"Until then I'll take a catnap. Wake me up when it's dragon-time."

Finn and Kathleen lay on the ice floe in their polar-bear capes. The uncanny night had fallen at noon, and a creeping mist had put out the few dim stars. Kathleen tried to keep perfectly still, tried to clench her jaws to keep her teeth from chattering, but she was torn by fear. She began to cry, soundlessly, without sobbing. Her tears froze and fell tinkling on the ice.

"What's that?" whispered Finn.

"My tears falling. They're frozen, and chiming when they hit."

"Why are you crying?"

"From fear. Aren't you afraid? I thought you were such a coward. Why aren't you afraid?"

"I've been a coward for a long time. I know how to handle it. Now stop weeping. The dragon will grow suspicious. Sleeping polar bears don't chime."

Kathleen stopped weeping, and waited for the dragon to come. Now Finn had warned her to lie there with her face hidden and not to look up. He didn't want her to see the dragon coming. He was afraid that the sight of it would so terrify the girl that she would call out and warn the dragon before he reached Finn, and that the monster would realize that he faced enemies, would pause to blow his breath on them, freezing their marrow and turning them into blocks of ice to be devoured at his leisure. So Finn had warned Kathleen to keep her eyes down and not to look up. But she found this very difficult. She heard a scraping slithering sound, and it grew louder, as if heavy chains were being dragged across the floe. She knew that the dragon was coming out of his cave and crossing the ice toward them.

She couldn't help herself. She had to raise her head and look. Then she wished she hadn't.

What she saw at first were two strange smoldering pits, far apart, but level, growing brighter and redder as they came toward her. She couldn't imagine what they were. But then, as the chain dragging grew heavier until the very ice trembled beneath her, she realized that these smoldering pits of light were the dragon's eyes. Then, by their light, she saw the whole terrible length of him—the huge snout full of teeth, the ridged spine, the great spiked tail. She heard its claws now scraping on the ice like enormous shovels, as the beast grew closer and closer. Finally, she couldn't stand it any longer. She let her head fall into her hands again with a little moan.

Then she heard a loud rasping snuffle which was its breathing, and she knew the beast was almost upon them, coming to inspect the two sleeping polar-bear shapes that were herself and Finn in their white fur mantles. She looked up again and, horror of horrors, saw its jaws gape, and snap up the white heap that lay beside her. She couldn't believe that Finn would be quick enough to slip out of the skin, but he did. In the glare of the dragon's eyes she saw the black shape of Finn's body crossing her. And then, an unbelievable roar, a mind-shattering rumbling howling cry was torn from the dragon, who practically stood on his tail in agony. She didn't dare rise to her feet. Simply curled herself into a ball and rolled away as fast as she could over the ice. She saw the dragon fall its full length, then scramble up and begin to beat its leathery wings with enormous force, and then rise into the air spouting flame like a volcano. And she knew the monster had swallowed the seeds of fire which were wrapped in the polar-bear skin, just as Finn had planned, and that there was a fire in its belly, and that it was in torment.

She watched in amazement as a huge gout of flame shot out of the dragon's mouth and touched an iceberg, lighting up the snow with radiant whiteness. She saw the iceberg hiss away in a giant plume of steam.

She tried to get to her feet then, but was flattened by the terrific downdraft of the dragon's wings as he beat them in his agony, flying in circles above the ice mountain. She struggled to her feet again, peering about for Finn, but she didn't see him anywhere. The dragon bellowed again, and spouted flame. And by its light she saw an unbelievable sight. Finn riding the dragon's head, a dagger in each hand, stabbing the leather skull first on one side, then the other, trying to steer the monster in its flight. She understood what Finn was

trying to do. Every time the dragon gushed flame the ice would melt and the sea would spring free. She understood then that Finn, riding the dragon's head, trying to steer it by dagger thrust, was using the monster as a giant flamethrower to melt the ice by which Vilemurk had locked the seas.

"Oh, grief," said Kathleen to herself. "He's a dead man. How long will he be able to ride that fearsome head? He'll be burned alive by the flame, or shaken free and gobbled up by the dragon, or lashed by that terrible tail. Good-by, Finn, unwilling hero, gray-eyed stripling of golden tongue. Farewell, my boy. . . ."

But she had no time for mourning. Finn had told her what she must do. She picked up his sword, and made her way across the slushy ice toward the mouth of the cave where Lyr lay bound.

Kathleen was right. Finn was in mortal danger. But he was in ecstasy too. There was something about being perched high in the air on this brute head, steering the monster with daggers, and watching the great streamers of flame melt the icebergs and crack the ice floes, and seeing the sea leap free—there was a glory about this that dissolved his fears just as the ice was melted by the flame. The great joy he knew then was a joy given very few men to feel, and those men are all heroes, of one kind or another. It was the joy a man feels when he turns one of the great keys of nature—which is usually far beyond any man's power—for Finn felt then that he, actually, himself, by his own efforts, by his own wit and daring, was changing the weather—unlocking the seas, restoring the life of its creatures, and rescuing from starvation those who draw their bounty from the sea. And when a man or woman feels that joy in turning one of nature's stubborn keys, then he is apt to forget all lesser pain, forget his fears, doubt, hesitation. He knows the ecstasy of being a great natural force. The winds blow through him, he is warmed by the primal flame, and for a brief moment, before he flares into death, he knows that he has melted the icy indifference that reality turns to man's hopes.

That is why Finn, who was no stranger to fear, as we know, kept riding the leather head, stabbing it this side and that with his daggers, steering the beast in its clumsy leather-winged flight so that the flame of its breath played over iceberg and ice floe, vaporizing the massy piles of ice, splitting the floes, and letting the green waters boil free.

So intoxicated was he with the joy of flight that he hardly realized it when the dragon, growing more accustomed to the savage flame in its belly, became aware of the lesser torment on its head, and snapped its enormous length like a whip, sending Finn high into the air. The dragon then did a half-somersault, pivoting upon its great wings, putting it in position to lash out with its tail at the falling body.

Now the air was thick with the steam of the melting icebergs, thick as soup. Finn saw the dragon turn, and poise its tail, and he knew what the beast intended. Falling as he was, Finn doubled up his legs and kicked out with all his might like a broncho sunfishing, and was able to lodge himself in a thicker column of steam, which was what he wanted. It slowed his fall somewhat, and partially hid him from the dragon. And the dragon struck too soon. The flailing tail missed Finn, but only by inches. He felt the point of its spike tear away his sealskin mantle, and the wind of the terrible lashing tail sent him blowing like a leaf, skittering sideways through the air. The force of it knocked him into a swoon. He fell onto a wedge of floating ice headfirst, and lay crumpled there, bleeding from the head.

He was plucked from the ice by a hungry mist-crone whose favorite fare in all the world was human blood—especially hero's blood, drunk fresh from the skull. She stooped low, chittering, and plucked him from the ice floe and flew away with him toward her nest. But then she felt his heart beating and realized that he was alive.

"I'd better not eat him," she thought. "He's worth more than a meal or two. He's a well-made young lad, and will make a fine slave for the smith demons. For such a one, no doubt, they will trade me ten worn-out old slaves, who, nevertheless, will furnish enough blood to last me through the season. Not hero's blood, to be sure, but we're in for a hungry winter, I know, what with Vilemurk's defeat. And it behooves me and my sisters to lay up stores where we may. The Master grows angry when the winter is warm, and the pickings will be lean, lean. . . ."

The mist-crone flew with Finn to the crater of a volcano in the dead middle of Vilemurk's secret domain. There she traded him for ten used-up smithy workers. Finn was taken down into the foul smoky depths of the mountain, and the mist-crone flew off, chittering happily, bearing a bladderful of fresh blood and a sack of fresh skulls.

Finn awoke to find himself a slave in the smithy, which is one of the worst things that can happen to anyone. The hollow mountain is a loathsome sooty place, lit only by the volcano fire, upon which the twisted smiths forge their weapons. The slaves are used to tend the fires and work the bellows, and haul the ashes, and scrub the anvil. They are kept half-starved, allowed almost no rest, and are worked until they drop. No guard is kept upon them because they cannot possibly escape. Each one is chained by the ankle to a round flat stone so heavy that the slave can barely trundle it along. Nevertheless, he is expected to keep up with his work. If he falls behind he is flogged almost to death. So the slaves drag their stones about from task to task as nimbly as they can. When completely worked out, and of no more use to the smithy, they are either fed to the flames or sold to the mist-crones, for the smith demons can always count on a fresh supply of slaves. Vilemurk makes constant war on the other gods, and on humans, and is always taking prisoners. And prisoners of war in those days were always enslaved.

At first Finn didn't care how soon he dropped from exhaustion and was fed to the flames. To labor ceaselessly in the strangling darkness, he thought, was worse than any death could be. He could hardly breathe, the air was so thick with charcoal dust and ash. And no matter how fast he worked he was beaten to make him work faster.

"Well," thought Finn to himself. "If it's time to go, I'll take one or two of them with me. The next time one of them starts to beat me I'll snatch the whip from his hand and knock out his snaggly teeth with its butt, and wrap the lash around his neck and strangle him with it. Then the others will bash in my skull with their iron mallets and that'll be that."

So he prepared for one last act of defiance, and immediate death. But then, for some reason or other, his wrath turned icy. His weird stubbornness arose, and his wits began to work.

"After all," he said to himself, "I've served an apprenticeship at suffering. All heroes must. Did I not, when still a small boy, fall into the clutches of the Fish-hag? And was she not a mistress of torments? Did her flying needle not sew up my lips and stab me into obedience? Did not the old witch herself work out on me twice a day with a whip that cut my flesh as cruelly as any of these? And my flesh was more tender then. And did I not bide my time and seek wise counsel from the Salmon, and learn to outwit the Hag, and leave her defeated—bound to a tree, humiliated? And didn't I make my escape then with full honors, and with her own tomcat, who has befriended me so well? And didn't I learn from her endurance, and the power of silence, and some of the arts of strategy? Am I to forget all that because of some weeks' discomfort? No! Finn McCool does not surrender so easily. He does not allow his enemies so easy a victory. His death will be dearly purchased. Let me think now. . . . Let me be true to myself and find a way out of all this misery, and pay back those who have made me suffer. That is the way of a man and a warrior."

And so, instead of snatching his few poor rags of sleep that night, he lay there in his grime and exhaustion, trying to make a plan. The next day at the forge, he spoke to the head smith, who was just putting an edge to a splendid sword, and said:

"Pardon, master, but that blade looks dull."

"What!" cried the smith. "Miserable earthworm! How dare you address yourself to me without permission. How dare you pass an opinion on a weapon I have forged? What do you know of swords anyway, slave?"

"Like many a slave," said Finn, "I was a warrior once, and the son of warriors. I am Finn McCool. My father was the great Cuhal. His sword, by common admission, was the finest ever forged. That blade could shear off a bull's horns or a boar's tusks as if they were twigs. I have seen my father scythe down an oak tree as thick around as a span of oxen with one whisk of that sword. I have seen him cut through rock. And I know for a fact, because the sword became mine upon my father's death, that it could cut through any link of any chain ever made. It was this sword that cut away Lyr's manacles when he was Vilemurk's prisoner, and set him free to turn the tide against your lord in his recent war. For I, myself, gave that sword into the hands of the one who struck the chains off the sea god."

"That was your sword?" said the smith wonderingly. "Your very own, the blade of Cuhal? We knew, of course, that it must have been that blade that cut Lyr free, for no other could have done it. We forged the manacles right here in this workshop. I forged them myself. As for the sword, I must tell you that it was made by my own father, who passed all his craft to me!"

"If you're as good as your father," said Finn, "why can't you make a sword as good as the one he made for my father?"

"It was not made for your father," said the smith. "It was ordered by Vilemurk himself to give as a gift to one of his favorites, the Prince of the North. It was stolen by your father."

"Not stolen. Taken as honorable booty from the hand of a dead enemy. My father, Cuhal, defeated the Prince of the North in a mighty battle, as you well know."

"Nevertheless," said the smith, "we have no call for such weapons these days. Vilemurk has ordered none that fine. But if he did, *I* would be the one to make it, I, I myself, son of my father."

"What do you mean there is no call for such a blade?" said Finn. "Does the call have to come from Vilemurk? Do you not hear your own pride speaking sometimes in the pulse of your blood during a sleepless night? Does it not say, 'You cannot prove that you are the man and the smith your father was—for you have done nothing to equal what he has done?' Do you never hear the teasing voice of your pride? Can you bear to live out your days in this smoky mountain laboring at these cheap weapons, never being able to prove that you have something special you can do? That you have a skill that can be matched by no other man or demon? For a skill unused is no skill at all. Your father might as well have taught his craft to that pillar of rock. For you have done nothing with it, and you will not be able to teach it to your son. It will have died of disuse."

"Stop it!" cried the smith. "Your words sting worse than those blind worms who gnaw at the roots of mountains and come through the rock at night to torment crater folk. Stop talking, I say! Not another word! Or I'll fling you into the fire straightway."

"You can stop me from talking," said Finn. "And you can fling me into the fire. But you will remember my words all the same, and they will burn in your mind. For I am only your own idea of yourself speaking. I am your thwarted pride speaking, and that you cannot silence until you do what you know you have to do."

"Enough," roared the smith. "I am as good a craftsman as my father. And I shall prove it . . . this very night. All night long shall I labor, and you will abide with me feeding the fire. And I shall forge such a blade as will make you forget the sword of Cuhal."

"Permit me to doubt it," said Finn politely. "I believe your talents have grown rusty through years of disuse, and that you will not be able to forge such a blade. But I will await the outcome with much curiosity nonetheless."

All night long the smith labored, bringing to his task all the cunning and all the lore learned by the mountain trolls through thousands of years of forging weapons since the first metal was smelted from the first ore dug out of the earth. For all that time, in an unbroken line, these helpers of Vilemurk, these twisted volcano demons, have been forging weapons for the gods, and for such heroes as have been able to steal them. And this smith was indeed a patient and clever craftsman. And he brought such a proud fury to his work that night as to go beyond his own skill and invoke a magic of craft beyond craft. All night long, Finn stoked the fire for him, and worked the bellows, watching closely, but keeping very still.

From a special bin the smith took a bar of volt-blue metal. This metal had been dug out of a meteor, which had flamed briefly in the sky centuries before, and then buried itself in the earth. After the meteor cooled, it showed a curious gray rock streaked with blue metal which the mountain trolls had taken as a prize. Only head smiths were allowed to work this metal from the sky, and only on the most special occasions. It was the hardest, most flexible metal in all the world, and took the sharpest edge. Finn recognized it—his father's blade had shone with the same silvery blue light—and his breath caught with excitement, but he was very careful not to show the smith how he felt.

The swordmaker heated the bar of metal red-hot, and plunged it into a vat of water until it cooled off. He did this three times, then heated it white-hot, and this time plunged it into a broth made of lion's blood to give the blade courage, and fox's blood to give it cunning, and owl's blood so that it would never sleep in its sheath— all mixed with crystalline ice water from the frost king's own fountain. Each time he worked the molten ingot, shaping it into a murderous elegant slenderness. Finally, on the forge lay a tapering two-edged blade, each of the edges honed razor sharp—and it came to a needle point. Before putting the final edge on it, however, the smith made its hilt. He twined leather strands about the rounded end of the blade. The leather had been cured from the hide of a new born bull calf; it was soft and very tough. Then he inlaid the leather with delicately spun gold wire. This combination of bull-calf hide and gold filament made a supple handle which could fit itself to any grip, and allowed the warrior to keep his hold on the hilt in the shock and ruck of the most violent battle.

The hand-guard was no simple crosspiece but a deep cusp made of brass leaf, beaten thin as flower petals and welded together leaf upon leaf, making a guard that was as supple as leather and tough as steel. No blade could shear through it to wound the swordsman's hand.

Finally, just as night ended, and the great gong sounded to call the slaves from their brief sleep, the smith honed the edge of the blade for the last time, wiped it down with an oily rag, and held it gleaming in the forge fire.

"Isn't it beautiful?" he said to Finn.

"Beautiful," said Finn. "As beautiful as the sword of Cuhal. But—can it cut as well? We must try its edge."

"Here," said the smith, thrusting the sword into Finn's hand. "You try its edge. You will find it can cut this anvil in two. And when you have satisfied yourself that it equals or surpasses the sword of

Cuhal, and that I, I am the author of this blade, I, and no other—why, then you will give it back to me and I will strike the head off your shoulders for your insolence."

"Well," said Finn. "I suppose it could be considered an honor to be decapitated by the best sword ever made—if such it is—but let me try it first before you finish your boast."

Finn made a pass or two in the air.

"Ah . . . nicely balanced," he said. "So far, so good. Now for the test."

But he did not strike at the anvil. He struck at his own ankle. As the smith stared in amazement, Finn struck off the chain which manacled him to the stone. He did a little dancing step, and laughed into the smith's face.

"Why . . . nothing makes you feel as light-footed as being chained to a rock for a couple of months."

"What are you doing?" whispered the smith in horror.

"Testing your sword. Indeed, it is everything you claimed. It cut fairly through my chains. I wouldn't be surprised if it were good at heads, too."

Before the smith could take a step backward, the blade glittered in the forge light once again, and swept the troll's head off his shoulders. And Finn himself, moving swiftly and silently as the shadow of flame upon the rock wall, fled up the hills of slag, up, up, up, his feet spurning the ash, and raising clouds of fine gray powder. Two sentries leaped to stop him. The blade flashed again, and two heads rolled in the ash. And Finn was out the mouth of the crater and rushing down the slope so swiftly he did not seem like a man at all, but like a goat leaping or a stone dropping.

Down the slope he rushed, down to the level ground, never breaking his stride. Onward he rushed, hurdling logs, leaping streams, into a girdle of trees. Through the trees, onto the beach. There, riding his luck, which is another name for hardship challenged and over-come, he spied a small skiff hidden in the reeds. It was a slender little coracle, made of hides stretched over wooden ribs—something like our canoes. He pushed it into the surf, jumped into it, and paddled away as swiftly as he could.

When he lost sight of land and knew that he was safe from pursuit, he stopped paddling, looked into the depths of the water, and said:

"O, great Lyr, God of the Sea, you whom I rescued from captiv-ity, O Lord of the Deep, I ask that you return favor for favor. Keep the sky fair and the waters calm, and give me a favoring wind that I may reach the shore of Ireland which I left so long ago. Any shore at all of the lovely land, I don't care. I'm no hard bargainer. Put me ashore at Leinster, Munster, Meath, or Connaught. I'll settle for any of them, and walk the rest of the way, rejoicing. But let the wind be fair. . . ."

No sooner had he spoken than the sky darkened. Black clouds roiled up out of nowhere. Lightning stitched the sky. Thunder growled. The winds pounced from all directions at once, spinning the skiff crazily. Finn flailed with his paddle on both sides, strug-gling to keep the little boat from overturning.

Then the last of the sunlight was snuffed like a candle. A howl-ing darkness fell. The skiff bucked like a wild horse Finn felt him-self going over. There was no way he could stop it. The coracle was turning turtle. He took a deep breath before going underwater.

The water was cold . . . cold. . . . He swam to the surface. He immediately flung himself in the direction he guessed the boat to be. He grasped its slippery side, hugged it tight with such force he thought its wooden ribs would crack, but he didn't dare ease his grip. The wind was trying to pull him off. Struggling with all his might, he succeeded in inching his way up on the overturned skiff, and sat astride it, gripping with his knees, clenching the keelson with his hands.

He had not lost his sword though, nor did he have to hold onto it. It seemed to press its length against his leg like something alive. Its metal seemed to glow warmly there with some sleeping fire from its comet birth. And it shone dimly, casting a small light so that he wasn't in utter darkness. When he grasped its hilt it was almost like grasping the hand of a friend. And, somehow, the dimly glowing, softly warming moon-metal sword kept him alive during that terrible night.

Dawn found him still clinging to the overturned skiff. Three-quarters drowned, punished by the wind, almost frozen—but still alive. It was a ghastly dawn. The sun stood on the horizon like a battered tin dish, and the sea was lead-colored. Then Finn saw the worst sight you can see upon the face of the waters—the long sleek bodies of sharks turning all around his boat, showing their white bellies and their triple row of teeth. They seemed in no hurry. They were trailing him, as if knowing there was no place he could go. But they came closer. There were seven of them, he saw, each one bigger than the next, and the smallest of them longer than his coracle.

"Looks like this is it all right," said Finn to himself. "But I wish I knew what's up with Lyr. He's acting as if I were his worst enemy instead of the one who traveled so many freezing miles to unlock his domain from the grip of Vilemurk. If he takes notice of me at all, it's not a friendly notice. For the sharks are subject to him, as are all the creatures of the deep. And, sure, they mean me no good at all . . . and they're getting closer and closer. Well, I won't make it easy for them."

The sword leaped into his hand. As one shark turned within arm's reach just under the surface of the water, Finn struck him with a slashing downward blow—and cut off the final length of him, as a fishmonger slices the tail off a bluefish before he wraps it in paper to give to a housewife. Blood dyed the water. Finn saw the wounded shark disappear under the snout-faced rush of the other sharks who converged on him, buried him under their threshing bodies, and in the space of half a minute had eaten him away to the bone.

"Wish I could say there was one less," said Finn to himself. "But there's a total of two more, because three new ones came to the feast."

He held his sword poised, but did not know which way to strike, for the sharks, with great intelligence, were now ringing the overturned skiff, and coming in from all sides, so that if he struck in one direction, the rest would be upon him before he could strike the other way.

"You're a lucky man, Goll McMorna!" shouted Finn. "The sharks are doing your job for you. And I will never face you now, sword in hand, to wrest the chieftainship of the Fianna from you. Farewell, Goll, farewell, enemy! Farewell, lovely little Murtha who lives in my memory. Farewell, Kathleen, most curious girl. Farewell, Fish-hag and Drabne of Dole, I'll trouble you no more. Farewell, Lyr, treacherous god. Farewell, Vilemurk. And now, a sharp farewell to you, my finny friends!"

Whirling the sword about his head, making himself a chaplet of blue fire for his final moments, Finn waited for the sharks to come.

Suddenly they were gone. He heard an odd gobbling, clucking sound, turned, and saw three enormous swans sailing across the water toward him. Huge birds, bigger than eagles they seemed, floating there. One swan rose to its knuckled claws and stretched its neck and beat its wings—and, far away, Finn saw the last of the sharks slicing through the water. The sun was still tin-colored, and the sea lead-colored, but where each swan floated was a pool of radiant blueness as if the birds carried their own light.

"There's some magic at work," thought Finn.

He was surer still of it when he felt himself being lifted gently in the air and the skiff righting itself beneath him, and himself dropping back into the seat of the coracle. The swan who had stood on its claws swam up to the boat. Its feathers flamed with such snowy brightness that Finn's eyes were dazzled, and he could not see. When his vision cleared, there was Kathleen seated in the skiff facing him. She wore a long lacy white dress that seemed to be spun of foam, and on her head she wore a crown of coral and pearl.

"We meet again," she said.

"Kathleen. . . ," whispered Finn. "You're more beautiful than ever. . . ."

"Easy now," said Kathleen. "Be very careful what you say. You're floating on Lyr's own sea, and there are things swimming all about underneath us who can hear every word, and are very ready to tattle."

"What are you talking about?" said Finn. "Lovely Kathleen, I'm so glad to see you. And you make less sense than ever. But thank you for chasing the sharks—for it was you, I know. And why are you sometimes a swan now? Tell me all."

"Be still then, and listen," said Kathleen. "Be doubly still so that you can hear me out and understand how our story ends. And also because that way you won't be uttering any dangerous words. I left you riding the dragon, and him spouting flame and melting all the icebergs. I never expected to see you again. But I did what you told me. I took your sword and crossed the melting ice and entered the mouth of the cave, and went down, down through the dark passageway, down the center of the mountain, attended by the tomcat who fought off the foul little trolls who attend Vilemurk down there. Down, down I went to where Lyr was chained to a great granite pillar.

"I lifted your sword and struck off the manacles. Just then the dragon must have passed directly overhead, and his flaming breath hit our ice mountain. All melted away in a cascading sheet of water. And Lyr, free again, floating on his own flood tide, with the ice melting all about him, the sea rising higher and higher—Lyr was king again, free and regal, trident in his hand, spearing the mist-crones and the frost legions and all his enemies—calling great blue whales from the deep who broached the surface of the sea, and fell with their tons of weight upon Vilemurk's allies.

"The battle didn't last long. Lyr rode the rising tide to victory. The ice was melted, and the seas were free again, and Lyr was king. I was swimming alongside him. Then I was riding his shoulder, clinging to his green beard. And . . . well . . . he was in a happy mood and full of power and joy—and grateful to me, I suppose, for striking off his chains. Anyway, he took me to his castle at the bottom of the sea, and made me his wife. One of them, that is. But his favorite, I guess. Unless . . . he's busier than even a god should be.

"So, in a kind of strange wet way I was a queen. Me. Kathleen ni Houlihan, daughter of my father who was lodged in his dung heap stinking up the east wind as it blew across Leinster. Well . . . I had never forgotten my father. Indeed, he's an unforgettable sort of man. So I craved a boon of Lyr. He sent a finger of the sea curling inland, and its cleansing tide swept away my father's midden. And a green salt magic turned my father into the cleanest creature in the whole world of living things—a swan. There he is now, that swan. See how white his feathers are. You would never know that he was once the dirtiest widower in the history of grief, would you? And that he had built up a muck heap of regret around him that was the shame of the four counties? No, he's a swan now. A big beautiful king swan. But he still has his angry red face. See?"

"And who's the other swan?" said Finn.

"Why, bless you," said Kathleen. "That's my mother. For

Lyr did me that favor, too. He called her back from the dead. Gods can do that, but they don't like to. Without that boon, however, the first one wouldn't have been any good—because my father would have refused to live as man or swan without his wife. There she is. Look at her. Isn't she beautiful? And this cleanliness now is no contradiction. For she was the cleanest little body anyone ever saw. So she comes rightfully by her feathers, and is very happy as a swan.

"Mother!" called Kathleen.

The smaller swan sailed over to the boat.

"I want you to meet my friend, Finn. It's him we owe everything to. He saved my life, you know—many times. And it was through him that I met Lyr. Greet him, Mother."

The swan spoke in a low throbbing voice, very much like Kathleen's, but gentler.

"Greetings to you, Finn McCool," she said. "Thank you for all you have done for my daughter and my husband and me."

She folded her white wings around his neck and pecked him softly on the lips.

"Thank you, madame," said Finn, "for the sweetest kiss ever bestowed upon a shipwrecked man."

"No sweeter than you deserve, Finn, who has rescued me from the dead, and my husband from the filth of despair, and made my girl a queen."

She pecked him again on the lips. Finn heard a strangled gobbling and looked up. He saw the largest swan rising onto his knuckled claws in the water, and beating his wings and shaking his red wattles furiously, and stretching his neck, and hissing.

"You there," gargled the swan who was Houlihan. "You there in the boat! What's that you're doin' with my wife. What's all this billin' and cooin'? What's the lout up to, darlin'? Is he trying to make free with you? I'll sink him so deep even the sharks won't find him."

He fluffed up his feathers so that he seemed to double in size, and swam slowly toward the skiff.

"Shut up, Dad," said Kathleen. "He's a friend of mine. And the best friend this family ever had. If it wasn't for him you'd still be on your dung heap, and I'd be long eaten by the dragon."

"Apologize to him, dear," said the mother swan. "Thank him for all he's done."

Houlihan clucked something unintelligible, and ducked his head underwater, pretending to fish.

"You're welcome, sir," said Finn.

The mother swan swam to her husband's side, and they both swam a distance away, and floated there, waiting for Kathleen. Finn said to her:

"What happened to Carth, who was your husband? Did you forget about him?"

"Oh, no," said Kathleen. "I worked a small magic there, too. He was too downy and gentle for a man—beaten too soft by his mother, unfit to be a husband. So I changed him into an aspect of his true nature. He's a downy duckling now, and my pet. He swims about with me sometimes, and I caress him, and feed him small fish, and he is very happy."

"And his mother?" said Finn.

"I changed her according to her nature, too. She's a pelican now. It made little change in her appearance, actually. I just pulled out her jaw a bit, and bent her nose a bit to meet it. And provided her with wings not unlike the sleeves of her dress. Her voice is the same. And she flies about croaking raucously, diving for fish. What's more, just to prove I have a kind heart, I gave her a final gift. An egg that will never hatch—really a stone, you know, from the bottom of the sea, but shaped and colored like a pelican's egg. She can sit on it in her nest, and sit, and sit, and it will never hatch, and never grow up —never fly away from its mother."

"Truly, you have a kind heart," said Finn. "And imagination to go along with it. I'm jealous of Lyr, Kathleen. I've never met a girl I fancied more."

"Hush now!" whispered Kathleen. "You fool! That's just the point. *He's* jealous of *you*. He knows our story. I told him the whole adventure, not realizing that his caprice is like the sea itself. And he's changeable as the sea, and as violent in his tantrums. He's conceived such an envy of you as to make your life unsafe whenever you venture near the water. I pray you, Finn, when I get you back to shore, try to stay there. Dry land's the place for you, lad . . . because the sea god is not fond of you."

"The next time the gods fight, I'll stay neutral," said Finn. "You help one of them against the other, and they both become your enemies."

And that's the end of this story. Kathleen changed back into a swan, and the three swans escorted the little coracle back to the shores of Meath, and Lyr did not strike again. But after that time Finn was very very careful whenever he found himself at sea. In fact, all his great victories were on land. He was never one for sea battles, because he was afraid he would lose.

Since that time, too, Kathleen ni Houlihan has figured in many legends. Sometimes she is said to be swan-born; sometimes she is known as the bride of the sea. Now we know why.

Since that time, also, dragons breathe fire.

Hanratty's Hunger

Through the years, as Goll McMorna had gone from success to success in Tara's court, he had made certain secret connections, who, for a fee, could be counted on for accurate prophecy, malicious counsel, and timely crime. Among these the most useful for the work at hand were none other than those dire sisters, Drabne of Dole and the Fish-hag. Goll did not know that they were acquainted with Finn, but they lost no time telling him.

It was a dark night when they met. He leaned against the bole of a cypress tree; they hung from a branch upside down, like bats, clutching the bough with their naked feet. Their full sleeves hung like bat wings, and their tangled gray hair hung. Their white eyes burned holes in the darkness. And they tittered like bats—teehee, teehee, teehee—for they considered it a joke to be summoned upon a midnight and paid for doing what they were most pleased to do—hunting young Finn.

"Teehee," tittered Drabne of Dole. "We know him well, my sister and I. He has played scurvy tricks on us both, yes indeed. Killed one of my slithery snakes and bribed the other. Snatched my crunchable little slave, the Thrig of Tone, from dearest vengeance mine. I remember. I remember."

"Did worse to me, to me!" shrieked the Fish-hag. "Ruined my Druid feast and disgraced me with the green-beards forever. Persuaded my charge, the Salmon of Knowledge, you know, to teach him certain forbidden wisdom. Stole my Salmon Net, caught and cooked the Loutish Trout, drugged my guests, abused me with the contents of my own sewing basket, and all in all made me suffer much. Too much."

"Doesn't sound too promising," said Goll. "He seemed like trouble a-plenty when I thought him only a little upstart. Now I learn that he has magical wits and strong allies."

"Oh, well, he has strong enemies too," said Drabne. "Namely us."

"He stole my black tom as well," said the Fish-hag.

"Hush, sister," said Drabne. "Let's listen to Goll. I believe he has a proposition for us."

"I have if you can handle it," said Goll. "Finn has performed certain tasks which make him think he's ready to claim the chieftainship of the Fianna. Of course, he must fight me first. And when I fight I like to win."

"Can there be any doubt about the outcome of such a battle?" said the Fish-hag. "Are you not the most fearsome warrior in the land? And Finn is still a lad."

"A precocious lad. . . ."

"So you do fear him?"

"Fear is a term I do not choose to recognize," said Goll. "But I respect anyone who offers to fight me. By overestimating my foe I find myself paying attention to detail. And it pays off, ladies, it pays off."

"So you wish us to take care of a few little details to ensure your victory?" said Drabne.

"Why not?" said Goll, grinning.

"In other words, you'd like him damaged a bit before the fight?"

"A bit. Or even quite a bit."

"How about your knightly honor and so forth?"

"That's for losers."

"You're a man after my own heart," said Drabne. "Or would be if I had one. Let's get it straight then. You'd like us to arrange some accident for Finn, preferably fatal."

"Preferably. I'd settle for a little less though."

"It's a large order. We'll need to do our very best evil in this matter, O man. It'll cost you something."

"How much."

"You know we wouldn't overcharge you—an old friend like you."

"I'm still listening."

"We have been in the habit of kidnapping certain infants from their cradles. But their mothers raise such a hue and cry, it's positively unsafe. Now we need these newborn babes. We need their skin for shoes when we go dancing. We need their bones to make buttons of, and their little hands for corpse-candles—which we sell to robbers, you know. When the fingers are lighted they cast a sleep upon all within the house so that the robbers may go about their business undisturbed."

"I can understand how mothers might object."

"Now what we want you to do is manage things so that we can pick up the brats and not be bothered by their mothers."

"Young mothers can be very unreasonable," said Goll. "How can I persuade them to ignore a threat to their newborn babes? You don't know what you're asking."

"Oh, yes we do. And we know what *you're* asking . . . which will cost you what we're asking."

"I don't know. . . ."

"You're a persuasive man, Goll. Find a way. Or we can't do business."

"I'll find a way."

"Now add several weighty bags of gold and we can reach an agreement."

"How many is several?"

"Loose term, is it not? Can mean as few as three, or as many as fifteen. Let us be moderate, however, and say twelve."

He groaned and smote himself on the head. But he knew better than to bargain with the crones. The longer the conversation, the more it would cost him. He groaned again, and said:

"Agreed."

"Go away, good customer," said Drabne. "Amuse yourself until the hour before dawn while my sister and I counsel together. When you return, we shall have a plan to present."

Goll strode away through the wood and left the withered sisters hanging upside down on their branch, twittering away to each other. How he would have liked to set a torch to them as he had done to wasps' nests when he was a boy. But he did not dare. He walked through the woods thinking many things, and returned an hour before dawn.

"Greetings, O Master of the Fianna," said Drabne. "My sister and I have conferred. We submit this plan."

Drabne spoke a long time then. Occasionally her sister broke in to add a detail or two. Goll listened very carefully. As he listened, he began to smile. When she had finished he was laughing. A curious sound, something like the creaking of a gate that has not been oiled; he was not used to laughing. When she was through, it was full dawn and he could see the witches in all their ugliness. He bit back his shudder. He knew full well that you must never show a female—young or old; maiden, nymph, or crone; filly, mare, or nag; chick or vixen; blooming girl or horrid hag—that she is anything but charming and desirable. He made himself smile, and kissed the withered claws of their hands, letting his lips linger on the mildewed hide, and said:

"Oh, sisters sage, your wisdom is surpassed only by your beauty. Truly, I thank you for this splendid strategy, and will begin the payment of your fee immediately."

"You are courteous indeed," said Drabne. "Quite our favorite client, in fact. Isn't he, sister?"

"Oh yes . . . oh yes . . . teehee. . . ."

"Thank you, kindly Crones," said Goll. "And farewell."

"Farewell. Do ill," they said politely, and flew away, blinking and smiling, for they hated the sun and loved the darkness.

Now, to understand the dreadful trap being prepared for Finn, you must know about Hanratty.

He was a king in Ulster, a huge burly brawling man. The battle-axe was his favorite weapon. There was no peace in Ulster, but there were long dull periods of truce when all he could use his axe on was trees.

One day he went farther than usual and found himself in a grove he had not seen before. Oaks grew there, beautiful thick old trees, evenly spaced. The earth was strangely clear of acorns and twigs, as if it had been swept. He did not know it but he had stumbled on a sacred grove of Amara, Goddess of Growing Things. All he saw was the thickness of the trees and a chance to use his wild strength. He stepped to the largest tree and raised his axe.

"Do not strike," the tree said.

"Why not?"

"This grove belongs to Amara. I am one of her oak maidens, grown old now, a priestess now, and this tree is her temple. It must not be defiled."

"This grove belongs to me," said Hanratty. "And I am not in the habit of consulting trees before I chop them down."

He swung his axe and buried its head in the trunk of the tree. The wind moaned through the leaves, and blood, not sap, bathed the axe-head. But Hanratty was used to blood; for a moment he fancied himself in the whirl of battle again, and happily swung his axe. By this time he was all spattered with blood like a butcher, but he chopped faster and faster—and the great tree fell with a tremendous crash. He looked at its bulk lying there, shouldered his axe and tramped away. Owls and hawks dipped in to sip the blood welling from the stump.

When Amara heard the news—and she heard it soon because birds are great gossips—she was torn by rage. Never had she been so insulted by mortal.

"No . . . I will not kill him, not just yet," she whispered to herself. "Death is too easy. I must think of something to fit the crime. And not in some dim afterlife, but here, right here on this earth he loves so well and uses so violently. Yes, I shall practice my reprisal on that big hot body whose pleasure he is always serving."

She paced her throne room, and thought and thought, and finally sent for one of her servants. This was a terrible servant, one she rarely employed, and only when people seemed to be losing veneration for the Queen of Harvests. The servant's name was Famine. She was not quite a skeleton. She had flesh, but it hung on her like rags on a scarecrow. Her lips had fallen away, and the fleshy part of her nose, and the flesh had been eaten away from her eyepits so that her face was four holes and a fall of hair.

"Hail, great Queen," she said. "It is long since you called upon my services. I have been in the Place of Shadow working for Oogah. She sends me out to frighten children. I come to them as dreams of their dead grandmother, bringing night-sweats and filial piety. Half-rations down there, Amara, half-rations. You see I have been forced to finish my own lips."

"I have a task for you, Famine. You will feed well for a while. . . ."

While this was happening, those dire sisters, Drabne of Dole and the Fish-hag, were preparing to strike.

Drabne of Dole, making herself invisible, followed Hanratty around his courtyard that noon, and stole his shadow. She folded it carefully, stuck it in her purse, and flew away.

That same morning, the Fish-hag went to the woodland pool where Finn swam each morning. She hid underwater and kept out of his way as he swam. Then she crouched under the bank and waited. He climbed out and knelt on the bank to look into the mirror of the still water and comb his hair. But as soon as his image flickered on the silver pool the Fish-hag seized it, stuck it in her purse, and swam off.

The sisters met in a clearing of the woods. They set a black pot boiling on a fire of twigs, and dropped in a frog, a spider, and certain magic spices. Then Drabne stirred in the shadow of Hanratty, and the Fish-hag added Finn's image she had stolen from the pool.

The pot bubbled; its lid bounced spurting steam. The sisters joined hands and danced around the fire, singing:

When we disagree
with nature's decree
Why, then, we two
simply brew
A magic recipe,
Or two, or three.
Teehee . . . tehee . . . tehee.

From the steaming pot two spites arose. Drabne seized one, spoke a curse, and hurled it northward. The Fish-hag seized the other, spoke a curse, and hurled it southward. The spites flew like darts, one toward Ulster, one toward Meath. They flew and darted and hurried and hurtled through the changing airs. One entered the castle in Ulster and bit Hanratty's neck, hanging there like a bat. The other found Finn as he was crossing a meadow in Meath, and bit him on the neck, hanging there like a bat. Hanratty fell to the floor, bloodless, and lay there with no more thickness than a cobweb. Finn's spite drank all his blood, and left the boy on the grass, no thicker than a cobweb.

A bitter draught blew through the castle, lifting Hanratty's cobwebby body off the floor, blowing it out the window, beyond the walls, southward. A sweet strong meadow wind blew, lifting Finn's cobwebby body off the grass and sailing it north.

Finn came to the castle, the king to the meadow. The lacy bodies plumped out, and took on color. But a powerful magic had been worked, making Finn and Hanratty change places. Finn now had Hanratty's appearance, and sat massively on his throne, while Hanratty was now a slender youth whose eyes were sometimes gray and sometimes blue as the light changed. They were still themselves in their souls, but with each other's body and habits—and both were in ignorance of the transformation.

And so it was that that night when Famine arrived to work Amara's vengeance she found Finn in Hanratty's place, and never knew the difference.

Finn had eaten and drunk himself into a heavy stupor, and was lying on his couch when he was visited by an amorous dream. A naked maiden, tall and graceful, came to his couch where he lay all flushed with wine. Her hands were cold, laving his heat. Cool as tall eels her drifting legs. And her hair seemed frosted. When he embraced her she pressed so close that the icy length of her body seemed to be entering his, laying delicious icy fingers on the very roots of his blood. He shuddered with pleasure, and slept.

When he awoke in the morning he was hungrier than he had ever been in his life before. He sent for a monster breakfast. Five huge melons. A great tureen of porridge. A baby pig, roasted whole. Twenty hens' eggs. And half a barrel of wine.

"Call that a breakfast?" he roared, flinging the barrel at the cook's head. "Food, man, food!"

The cook was terrified. The king had eaten all his own breakfast, and his daughter's breakfast, and the servants', too. But still he called for more. Even in the kitchen they could hear him bellowing —all the way from the great dining hall. Nothing to do then but to serve him what had been planned for lunch. Now they brought him a huge haunch of venison. A peck of potatoes roasted in their skins. Also pastry, honey, apples, grapes. And a barrel of undiluted wine.

They brought him food. Finn sat at the great table, roaring with hunger, striking the board with the haft of his axe. Hanratty's young daughter sat near him, not daring to speak a word, staring at the man she thought her father, amazed. Finn seized the haunch of venison as if it were a drumstick and ate it swiftly, wrenching the

meat from the bone, eyes bulging. When he had stripped all the meat away, he cracked the head of the huge bone between his teeth and sucked the marrow. Then he reached with both hands, seizing potatoes and pastry and fruit and shoving them indiscriminately in his mouth, chewing and mumbling, and looking about the table for more. He ate the fruit—skins, pits, and all—drained the flagon of honey, then raised the barrel of wine to his mouth, drank that off, and flung the barrel away.

The girl was still staring at him.

"You know, you're very pretty," he said to her.

"Father, what's the matter? Why are you looking at me like that? Don't you know me?"

"You must be my daughter since you call me father."

"But why are you acting so strangely?"

"Pretty girls shouldn't ask questions. They should enjoy their food, and smile, and play the harp."

"Would you like me to play, Father? And sing for you?"

"After we've had something to eat. I must apologize for this meager fare, my dear. . . ."

"Are you still hungry, father?"

"Cook!" he bellowed. "Where is that rascal?"

The servants rushed to the storeroom to get what was laid by for dinner. A very lavish state dinner—he had planned to entertain three kings. But his daughter told the servants to prepare the food as quickly as they could, and she herself sent messages to the three kings, asking them to come another time.

So the great kitchen fires blazed. Spits were turning. Pots were boiling. Every servant was working like ten. For it was not enough to prepare the dinner. Finn still sat at the table, and they had to assuage his raging hunger by a constant stream of tidbits until the main course should be ready. But they could not appease him. He came storming into the kitchen and seized a half-cooked sheep from the spit, and ate it right there, standing in front of the fire, feet spread, one hand on each end of the spit, not noticing that his hands were burning. He devoured the sheep, and cracked the bones and sucked the marrow—and smote the cook again for being slow. Then he went back to the table to wait for his meal.

The bewildered footmen tried to serve him as if it were a formal dinner and he a banquet room of guests. They began with a huge carp, which had been raised in the royal pond and fed only on swans. He didn't bother to slice it. He ate it from tail to nose, crunching the bones, eating the eyeballs like grapes. Then he ate several giant crabs, shells and all. He drank off a tub of mutton and barley soup, then went to work on a whole roasted ox stuffed with pigeons. When he finished the ox it was midnight. His eyes were glazed, his face red and swollen. But he ate the honey and cakes and fruit, finishing another barrel of wine—and then, finally, stumbled to his couch with a bowlful of walnuts. And the weary servants who had been feeding him since dawn began to clear the table.

He awoke in the middle of the night, ravenous. The servants were all asleep. He would have roused them, but he couldn't bear the delay. He took a torch and went to the kitchen. The cupboards were bare, not enough there to interest a mouse. He went to the storeroom, placed the torch in a sconce on the wall, and then looked at the carcasses hanging from meat hooks. He lifted an enormous side of beef from its hook, sat down on a barrel and began to devour it. It wasn't cooked, of course, but he didn't care. By dawn all the carcasses were gone—the oxen, the sheep, the dressed goats—he had eaten them all. He went off to take a nap before breakfast.

By the end of the week there wasn't a scrap of food to be found in the castle or in any of the houses around. The villagers had fled—because he had sent his soldiers to take their livestock. He hunted from morning till night. Game was plentiful. He killed stags and wild boars, nor did he fear to hunt the savage bear, for bear steaks were good too. But, mighty hunter though he was, he could not kill enough each day to satisfy the day's hunger. Famine was inside him; when he fed himself he fed her. And she grew stronger and stronger and made him want more and more and more.

Finally, his kingdom was swept bare. The villagers had fled; their crops lay untended; he had devoured all their stock. There was no game in the forest, no fish in the rivers. He sold all he owned—his castle and his jewels, his very crown, his chariots; the horses had long been eaten. He sold everything, keeping only his battle-axe. Then he took the princess and went to another kingdom to buy food with his gold. It was a treasure of gold, a huge leather bagful. But inside a week he had spent it all on food, and had nothing left.

Now the hunger began to torment him so that he could think of nothing else. More than a hunger, it was more like a thirst, but for food. A thirst, parching every juice of his body, involving all his organs, squeezing his entrails into one burning mandate—food!

Finn was walking outside the city, along the shore, trying to find a washed-up fish, upending rocks and scraping barnacles off with his teeth, for they had tiny specks of flesh inside. Gulls stooped, screaming. He was hoping to catch one. A man of the city passed, walking by the shore. Stout, richly dressed, a merchant by the look of him. He passed, and looked back again at Hanratty's daughter.

"Stop!"

The man turned. Finn held the girl by the wrist, and walked to the merchant.

"You, there. You looked at her."

"I meant no offense, sir," said the man.

"I don't care what you meant. Do you like her?"

"What?"

"This girl, man, the girl. Do you fancy her?"

"She is . . . very beautiful."

"How beautiful?"

"What?"

"How beautiful? In money? How much?"

"Are you offering to sell her?"

"She's mine to sell."

"I hesitate to name a price."

"Don't hesitate."

"I'm not a rich man. . . ."

"Look, sir, I am a king, no greasy merchant. I do not bargain. I am a king and I am offering you a princess. The price is ten bars of gold, which I know you can afford. So let us conclude before I lose my temper."

The merchant looked at the huge hairy wild-eyed stranger, and then at the lovely young girl. He sighed deeply, and wrote an order for ten bars of gold. Finn snatched the paper and rushed toward the city to the countinghouse before it should close. The merchant and the girl stood looking at each other on the beach.

She was looking at him, but her eyes had already veiled over, refusing to see him. She had seen enough in one swift glance—the mild pouting cheeks, the tiny mouth, the shrewd eyes, the big stomach. She moved from him and waded out into the water, and stood there, whispering:

"Oh, Father Lyr, you whom I have always honored above all the gods—ever since I was a little girl and my father thrust me into the salt bay like a wriggling little tadpole, and I felt no fear at all, only a wild bliss—oh, Lyr, whose sea I have always loved, whom I love even in rage because your rage is storm and in the center of storm I find silence which my heart drinks—O Lyr of the living waters, oh, master of the horse, swinger of tides, hear my prayer. I am only a young girl, a lost princess whose father, the king, has gone mad. Please, please deliver me from the gross body of this transaction. Please, please save me from this ugly old man. At his touch I will either perish, or kill him and go mad as my father. Please help me, Lyr, and teach me to help my father in his crazed hunger."

The merchant stood there on the beach keeping an eye on his new purchase as she stood knee-deep in the water. Then he saw a wave rolling, larger than the others. Even as he looked upon it, its cusp deepened and seemed to fill with hot silver. The light was too bright; it stabbed his eyes with pain. He looked away and blinked— and, when he looked back again, there was no girl there, but a fisherman casting his net.

"Fisherman, fisherman," he cried, "have you seen a girl?"

The fisherman shook his head silently.

"Where is she, where did she go? She's brand-new—just finished paying for her. Where did she go?" He raced down the beach, frantically looking for the girl.

That night, Finn was in the hovel where he now lived, finishing an enormous meal, when he saw an old fisherman come in with a net over his shoulder. He threw the net on the table and little silver fish spilled out.

"For your breakfast," said the fisherman, and turned into Hanratty's daughter.

"A clever trick," said Finn. "Where did you learn it?"

"When you left me with that terrible man, I prayed to Lyr to help me. He did. He taught me sea changes."

"Think you can do it again?"

"Oh, father. . . ."

"Well, if Lyr is trying to help, let him do it right. Gods should not stint—any more than kings. You just keep saying those prayers, missy. I see a small but steady income."

The next day he sold her to a landowner. When the old man tried to embrace her, she turned into the likeness of his wife, paralyzing him with fear. And so she slipped away.

Then she was sold to a hunter. She turned herself into a dainty little red fox and led his hounds on an exhausting chase—and when they came near, called to them in her own voice. They were confused, so was the hunter. In the confusion, she slipped away.

A sailor bought her next. When he tried to come close, she leaped overboard, turned into a seal, and swam away more swiftly than he could follow.

Finn kept selling her and she kept changing into other shapes, and returning to him to be sold again. And he was able to keep himself in food, but his hunger grew and grew. Finally, it was necessary for him to sell her everyday; it took that much gold to buy the food he needed.

One day she was late returning. He grew ravenous, and went striding out of the hovel, axe poised, looking for something to kill. A cat crossed his path. He swooped and caught it. It was an orange cat, sleek with good eating, because it used to meet the fishing boats coming in, and was thrown scraps by the fishermen as they gutted the fish. She didn't bite or scratch, but settled herself in Finn's hands, almost purring. She was used to men. Finn gloated upon her fatness, and was ready to devour her—fur, claws, whiskers, and all. His fingers tightened about her neck. She looked him full in the eye. A shaft of green fire pierced the man, making him cry out in puzzled grief. He forgot his hunger for a moment, and almost remembered something else. He heard a voice being wrenched from him, a different voice from the one he'd been using, a younger voice. He heard it calling,

> Creature pair of earth and air,
> Here and there, and everywhere
> Come, I pray, and serve me fair.

He heard wings beating and the wild cry of a hawk screaming its joy. He saw a black shape hurtling toward him along the beach, and heard the pleasured yowl of a tomcat. And the hawk, Finn's own falcon, landed on his shoulder. And the huge black tomcat he had taken from the Fish-hag rubbed against his leg, purring hoarsely.

"Oh, master," cried the hawk, "we've been looking for you everywhere."

"Yes-s-s," said the cat. "And now we've found you, and shan't lose you again."

Unhesitatingly they had recognized their master, Finn, within the gross uniform of Hanratty's flesh. For when animals love you they can see beyond appearances. And in their knowledge of him Finn began to remember things. Slowly, painfully, he began to untangle his mind from its sleep of greed.

"Who are you?" he cried. "Who am I?"

"You are Finn McCo-o-o-l, son of Cuhal, chieftain-to-be of the Fianna," said the cat. "Stolen from us by enchantment laid upon you by my old mistress, the Fish-hag, and her sister, Drabne of Dole. Made to change forms with a mad king of Ulster, Hanratty by name, who offended Amara, Goddess of Groves, and was punished by her with Famine. . . . Except she punished you instead, thinking you the wicked king."

"Oh, what a mixed-up tale," cried Finn. "So many puzzles, so many enchantments, so many crimes and mistakes. My head reels!"

"Easy. . . ." said the hawk. "Easy, young master. Puss there never did know how to tell a story. Blurts it all out in one big undigested lump. Let me tell you one thing at a time, so that we can begin to undo the evil. You are under enchantment. We must disenchant you in some way. Then we can begin to think about vengeance, and so forth."

"Hanratty has my body, you say? And this is his?"

"Right," said the hawk.

"That girl—she's Hanratty's daughter?"

"She is, poor lass."

"Poor lass, indeed," said Finn. "Well, my friends, let us counsel together. I want to be me again—and soon."

"We have already given some thought to this matter," said the cat. "And even have made a bit of a plan. But I'll let the hawk tell you; she puts things so much better."

"Thank you," said the hawk. "Our plan is simple. To capture the Fish-hag, and force her to concoct a reverse spell that will put Hanratty back into his body here, with all its awful cravings, and you back into yours. While I have been given the honor of telling you the plan, our friend, the tomcat, has reserved for himself the glory of its execution. Since he knows the witch's habit and has some experience in magic, it is he who will hunt her down and do what must be done. As for me, I will stay here and find you food, which seems to be an assignment large enough for anyone."

"I am so happy to see you two again that I can hardly speak," said Finn. "I want to weep. But I won't do that, either. Just take my thanks, good friends."

"Farewell," said the cat. "I go hag-hunting."

"And I," said the hawk, rising in the air, "will just go hunting. . . ."

Now the cat had kept very close watch on the Fish-hag since the hour he had learned that it was she and her sister who had done a mischief to Finn. He had gone to the Salmon Pool, prowled the hazel copse, blending into the shadows of the trees as only a black cat can —and then, at night, prowled outside her windows, peering in, leaping on the roof, listening to all that went on. At first he could find no way to surprise her. Then she gave him his chance.

She took to entertaining an extremely important Demon of Darkness, who came a-wooing in his favorite form—a rat. But a very handsome rat. A huge pearl-gray one, larger than a rabbit, with black

ears, and black tail, and silky jet-black whiskers. Now the cat had
seen her receive many swain in the years he had spent with her, but
never had he seen her so frantically in love. At first she welcomed
him in her own form, but found that a bit awkward, and of late had
changed herself into a she-rat for his visits, which they both found
more convenient. She was a suave brown rat with dainty paws and hot
golden eyes. The cat thought she looked much better this way. And
he kept watching, kept planning . . . so that when he and the hawk
were overjoyed one afternoon to hear Finn's voice dimly calling over
hundreds of miles, over sea and plain and forest, speaking the old
magic rune—when they had heard the beloved voice of their vanished
master and had answered its call, why by that time the cat's plan was
ready for action. And now he was on his way back to the hazel copse.

What he did is soon told. He waited until night came, and
blended into the shadows—ghosted through the window, and the
Hag never knew he was there. He waited in the corner and watched
her weave a small spell, and turn herself into a pretty brown rat. She
hopped on a cushion and folded her paws demurely, waiting for her
demon lover.

But it was the cat who came. He pounced.

"Good evening, mistress," he said, holding her fast, fixing her
with his blazing green eyes, grinning at her with his successful teeth.
"It is long since we met, you and I. But you haven't been idle all that
time, have you? Oh, no. You've been busy, busy, busy . . . doing
jobs for Goll McMorna, have you not? And one special job . . .
which involved the disappearance of my master, Finn."

"I can tell you where he is," gasped the Fish-hag.

"Oh, I know where he is. And I know what you must do to
escape being very thoroughly chewed and eaten." He sank his claws
deeper into her hide, and shook her gently, and murmured, "Do you
know?"

"Yes . . . yes . . . ," said the Hag. "At least I can guess. Please don't eat me. I'll do anything . . . anything. . . ."

"Well, you must do exactly as I say, and not try any of your tricks." And he bit off her tail to show he meant business. She screamed and struggled but he held her in his claws. "Be quiet," he said. "Or I'll lose my patience entirely, and gobble you up in a one-two-three. . . . And wait here and do the same for your friend, the gray rat, when he shows up. You can hold a touching reunion in my stomach."

"No . . . no . . . ," moaned the Hag. "Don't eat me, please don't —just tell me what you want me to do. Above all, don't kill him, the darling."

"I want you to undo the spell whereby you made Finn and Hanratty swap bodies. I want them both restored to their own forms, and I want that to happen in the next three minutes."

"It will, it will, I swear. Just lift your paw a bit, that's a sweet dear puss. I'm suffocating."

Back on the beach of that northern county of Eire called Ulster, Finn, still lodged in Hanratty's body, had just eaten a meal of mutton —for the hawk had caught him a sheep. The meat lay heavily upon his stomach, and his mouth felt greasy. He was weary, weary, weary of inhabiting Hanratty's flesh. Now that he knew who he was again he longed for his own lithe form.

Then, suddenly, he found himself changing. He was standing on the shore. Small waves were hissing in the moonlight. He felt himself growing lighter, lighter. The terrible heavy bestial stupor lifted from his brain too, and from his heart. The gnawing hunger was gone from his belly—in fact, his huge belly had gone.

He laughed with joy. He was himself again. Finn McCool. With a glad shout he dashed into the ocean and clove the ice-cold waves, welcoming the icy shock, feeling himself being scrubbed of lardy Hanrattiness—feeling all the filth and sweat of his brutish greed washing away. He came out of the water and danced on the beach. The hawk circled low and flapped her wings in time to Finn's singing. A thicker shadow fledged out of the blackness and joined them—the tomcat. He stood on his hind legs and danced in the moonlight too.

"Welcome home!" screamed the hawk. "You did a noble job."

"She kept her promise, the Hag," said the cat. "But it took a wee bit of persuasion."

"Thank you, cat! Thank you, hawk," cried Finn.

Suddenly fatigue hit him. He fell dead asleep right there on the beach. The hawk folded her wings and slept. The cat curled up close to Finn and slept.

In the morning Finn swam again, and studied himself in a trapped bit of high tide that made a pool.

"Oh, my," he said. "Hanratty had the loan of my body only a few months but he's left it in terrible shape. I'm in no condition at all to fight Goll. Yet fight him I must. It's time and high time. I must go into training immediately. Where *is* Hanratty, by the way?"

"Somewhere near," said the hawk. "Prowling the beach, looking for food. Selling his daughter. When he resumed his body he took on its hungers. Famine is in him—even more pitiless now."

"Well, I guess I'd better settle with him first. I've formed a violent dislike for the fellow. I'll settle with his daughter too, the lovely one. Perhaps, if I serve her well, I may finish off the father too."

Whistling happily, he went looking for the princess. A bit later Hanratty's daughter found herself speaking to a strange young man. She was puzzled by his eyes. She couldn't tell if they were blue or gray; they kept changing.

"How can I pay for you?" said the young man who was Finn. "You are beyond price."

"Thank you. But a price will fetch me just the same."

"I have no money, my dear."

"But you look rich."

"Just habit. Means nothing. I have no money, and never mean to make any. Nor should I expect anyone to give me any. Because I do nothing."

"Nothing?"

"Oh, well, I have done certain things. I have fought an enemy or two, broken a horse, killed a boar, made a song. . . . But I cannot return to these things except as a pastime. For I have sworn an oath never to make money out of what I enjoy. So I shall never be able to afford you, and must bid you farewell."

"Seems a pity," she said.

"A great pity. In fact, I don't quite know how I'm going to bear the pity of it because the more I look at you the more beautiful you are, and the harder it is for me to say farewell. Nevertheless, I have no more money now than when I began that sentence. All I can suggest is that you offer yourself to me free, then I'm sure we could come to some arrangement."

"I cannot."

"Why not?"

"I need the money."

"What for? Why do you need it more than I do? Can either of us buy anything more than we are offering each other?"

"I need it for my father, that man over there."

"He allows you to sell yourself?"

"He encourages it."

"Beautiful daughter like you—I don't see how he can bear to part with you for love or money. Is he really your father?"

"Yes."

"What a wild desperate look he has, to be sure. I have no money to give him, but I have promises. I think he should believe them. Desperation feeds on promises."

"They'll never feed him. He needs more solid fare than that."

"Well—no harm in trying."

Finn strolled over to Hanratty, and said:

"Good day, sir. Your charming daughter and I have been trying to strike a bargain. I would gladly give all I have for her—which would be easy because I have nothing."

"I don't do business with paupers," growled Hanratty. "Get out!"

"Ah, you won't want to be sending me away before hearing what I have to say. For I do have prospects, you know. My parents are very rich, and both are on the point of death. Tomorrow should see them safely—I mean unfortunately—on their funeral pyres. Let me have the girl tonight, and tomorrow you shall have your money. Plus a bonus for prompt delivery."

Hanratty stared at the young man. Then he called his daughter aside and spoke to her in whispers—insofar as he could squeeze his great raw voice into a whisper. He told her what Finn had said.

"What do you think?"

"I don't know, Father."

"Would you believe him, if you were I?"

"If I were you, I should not have to believe him. I should not be selling my daughter."

"Never mind that. Don't start that now. Do you think he'll come up with the money?"

"I know nothing about him."

"He promises a big extra fee if I trust him."

"No doubt."

"You don't think he's to be trusted?"

"What do we have to risk, after all? Under the circumstances your merchandise remains intact. I shall return to you whether he pays or not."

"Yes—but we may waste a whole day. And food is getting very low. I can't waste a day. If you don't trust him we'll find another buyer."

"Perhaps I'd better go with him. It's the only way to find out. If he seems unable to pay, or unwilling, why then I will change my shape straightaway, and come home to you. And only a few hours will be lost. It's worth the risk."

"I suppose so. All right, young fellow!" Hanratty shouted. "She's yours. But I expect to see the color of your gold tomorrow or you'll wish we had never met. I am no man to fool with."

"Indeed not, sir. By tomorrow you shall have all that's coming to you."

Finn took her to a hut in the hills. She looked around swiftly, seeing what windows there were, how big the chimney was—for the exits determined the shape of her transformations. But her appraisal was not cool this time. He was standing too close. Moving very swiftly and softly he took her into his arms. She immediately turned herself into a cat, a large white one. But she was still in his arms. Calmly he sat down on the bench in front of the fire and held her on his lap—too tightly for escape, not enough for pain—held her, and tickled her under the chin, and stroked her fur the right way from nose to tail, muttering softly: "What a lovely little animal you are." And to her horror, she felt her eyes closing, heard herself beginning to purr.

And even as he was stroking her, she turned herself into a porcupine. She heard him gasp with pain, felt his grip loosen, and she began to slip away.

"Pretty sharp," he said. He flipped her over, and seized her where there were no quills. And held her, speaking softly.

"Let's see what else you can do," he whispered.

She turned into a crow, but he held her by the wing and admired her feathers. She turned into a snake. He held her about the middle and told her how beautiful her eyes were, how gracefully she entered a room. Through all her changes he kept holding her and would not let her go. And she realized she would have to become something that could kill him, and changed herself into a she-bear.

He bowed to her, smiling, and said: "Shall we dance?"

She grunted and took him into her fatal hug. She crushed him against her, feeling the glad bestial strength surge, wanting to break him and forage among his bloody bones; and suddenly she understood her father, understood the wild greed, and how you need to take into yourself what you desire.

She hugged Finn closer, and saw her arms growing pale. Felt all her decisions slipping away inside, all her changes dissolving. And now it was he who was crushing her. She was clinging to him —in her own form—a bearskin swinging from her wet shoulders. She looked up at him.

"Where did I get this fur coat?" she murmured.

"I gave it to you," he said. "It belonged to a bear I killed. It looks better on you."

"Do you think I'm beautiful?"

"Well, I think, all told, this is your best disguise."

"Do you love me?"

"I've always liked variety. Have we finished our charades for this evening?"

"Yes. . . ."

The next morning Hanratty waited and waited, but his daughter did not come. He went to the beach. A gull dipped, and he thought it must be she—but it screamed and flew away. A fish leaped and he thought it must be she, but it didn't come up again. All day he waited, and she did not come. He spent his last coins on food, and raged with hunger all night thinking she must surely come the next day. But she did not.

He was mad with hunger. He felt that unless he had a huge meal immediately he would seize a child off the road and eat it. He had no money left, and nothing to sell except his battle-axe. So he traded it to a farmer for a thin cow—and killed her with a blow of his fist in the next field, and ate her raw—horns, hoofs, and all. He went back to the beach. His daughter did not come.

Hanratty waded out and tried to catch a fish with his hands. He almost caught a large one, but it slipped through. He roared with disappointment and shook his fist at it. He saw the balled meaty hand moving in front of his face—and his other hand moved by itself, lashed out, caught the fist, and pulled it to his mouth as it struggled like a little animal. But he held it still, and bit off his thumb. It was tough and gristly, but he ate it with great relish, gaining strength from the food, and greed from the strength—and before he knew it he had snapped off all the fingers of one hand. Then he ate the fingers off his other hand. He looked at the bleeding stumps and thought dully: "Now I won't be able to hold my food properly." And, still ravenous, he ate his left arm up to the elbow.

He squatted on the beach. Hunger burned more savagely than ever. He was drunk on the smell of his own blood, but he felt an odd dazed comfort; he no longer had to seek food—it was right there for him now until the end of time. And, squatting there, grunting, slavering, he slowly devoured himself, stretching his neck until it was as long as a serpent's and he could reach all the farthest parts of himself. He ate steadily—until all that was left was his mouth, which smiled greedily and swallowed itself.

It was dawn now. The gulls were screaming, trying to wake the fish. An old Hag with ashy hair and bloody lips stood on the beach where the king had been. She cackled once, rose into the air, and flew away through the dodging gulls.

At the hut in the hills, Hanratty's daughter and young Finn McCool had risen early too, being very hungry, and were eating breakfast on the bench in front of the fire.

Finn and Goll

N ow Finn sought Goll McMorna to challenge him for the chieftainship of the Fianna. He journeyed across Meath, harp slung. It was a blue smoky fall day. The cat stalked after through the grass; the hawk circled low. They neared Tara, castle of the High King, where Goll also dwelt, and Finn watched eagerly for the first sight of its white stone walls and its roof, striped crimson and blue. But no castle appeared. They had come to a wall of fog, but not like any fog they had known; it did not move upon the wind, nor rise, nor thin away. When they tried to pass through they did not bump into anything solid, but simply lost the power of movement until they stepped back.

"What is it?" cried Finn.

"Nothingness grown solid," said the harp. "A clot of that which is not barring that which is. Different forms of not-ness mixed, perhaps—invisibility, silence, denial—who knows what angry gods build with. Beyond it lies Tara, or where Tara used to be."

"You think this the work of angry gods?"

"Or playful ones. They're equally dangerous."

"What do we do? How do we pass?"

"Hard questions. We cannot seek their answer in ordinary places. Say a verse—quickly! Touch me and sing!"

Finn touched the harpstrings, and sang:

> Harp on tree,
> Hawk to sea,
> Cat makes three.

"I read it like this," said the harp. "You must hang me on a tree. The winds will come telling what they see when they blow over Meath. And you must send the falcon flying to question the fowls of air. Set the creepy cat crawling in the underbrush, seeking rats and such as live in holes and burrows, going in and out and are filthy and have information. We shall gather the news and bring it back."

"Away with you, friends!" cried Finn. "And I shall study this puzzling wall more closely."

The hawk flew away to question the gulls, as instructed. The cat vanished into the underbrush. And Finn hung the harp on a willow tree.

He, himself, departed to circle the wall of fog and look for a way through, but he came back to where he had started without glimpsing Tara. He came to the willow tree where he had hung the harp. It swayed there in the wind, singing softly. The hawk sat on a branch near it, and the cat sat next to the hawk.

"I found no way through the fog," said Finn.

"Nor will you," said the harp. "Listen, Finn, to what we have learned, we three. It is a magic fog, sowed by a hundred mist-crones flying in formation. They were sent by Vilemurk to hide Goll Mc-Morna from you and prevent your challenge. And, it is said Goll will stay hidden until Vilemurk cooks up a tactic that will assure your defeat."

"Things don't seem to be going so well," said Finn.

"Not well at all, my boy. You need some influence in high places too, or you will never get to lead the Fianna. All you'll be leading is your own funeral procession."

"What shall I do?"

"Seek the help of a god."

"I seem to offend every god I meet. Vilemurk is my declared enemy, of course. And you know what Lyr thinks of me because of Kathleen. And that episode with Hanratty's daughter didn't help me there either. Lyr had his eye on her too. She appealed to him once and he taught her sea changes. I don't know any god who'll help me."

"Try a goddess then. You seem to do better in that direction."

"What goddess?"

"Amara, Queen of the Harvest. She owes you a favor anyway. She hit you with Famine instead of Hanratty. An accident, of course, but you did suffer in her cause. It's worth a try. You have nothing to lose."

"Come then," said Finn. "We'll look for Amara."

He found her under an oak tree, picking acorns. It was the largest oak in Eire, perhaps in the world. Unimaginably old, with a huge bole, massive limbs, and deep ridged bark. It was called the Druid's Oak, and was Amara's favorite place.

She was so tall she could stand under the oak and put fallen birds back into the nest merely by reaching her arm. Clad in green she was; her hair hung thick and yellow as sheaves of wheat. As Finn approached he became aware of the fragrance arising from her bare shoulders; she smelled of sunshine and crushed grass. Her beauty robbed Finn of his sense; he could hardly speak.

"Do you seek me, lad?" she called.

"I seek you, O Queen of the Harvest. I seek your favor."

"Speak."

"Unwittingly, you have done me harm."

"Do you dare come to Amara with reproaches? I cherish only what grows. Where there is blame nothing grows."

"I am grateful for the injury you did me, lovely goddess, since it leads to our acquaintance."

"What injury? Who are you?"

"I am Finn McCool whom your servant, Famine, mistook for Hanratty, whose form I had been forced to take by enchantment."

"Oh, yes, Hanratty . . . the grove-defiler. I'd almost forgotten."

"It was I who was entered by Famine. I suffered the torments of hunger, and the worse torments of gluttony."

"What of Hanratty? Did he go free, that foul butcher?"

"Only at first. I was released from enchantment, and we resumed our own forms. I wooed his daughter, and Hanratty disapproved of the match—and ate himself up alive."

"A proper ending," said Amara.

"Proper indeed. Now I go in search of my enemy, Goll McMorna. But he is being aided by Vilemurk and I need help in high places. I come to you, Amara, whom I love and honor beyond all other gods and goddesses."

"You want my help?"

"Yes."

"Do you not know that a god's favor can damage a weak man beyond repair—that it can twist him and shake him and blast him till it seems like a curse?"

"Ah, lady, I am accustomed to risk. And I have already been blessed or cursed by the sight of your beauty. I will take all you have to give, if you do the giving."

"You will obey me in all things?"

"I will."

"Stand there then, and accept what comes."

She stretched her arms high. Her tall radiance blotted the weak sunlight. The afternoon was stunned by her beauty. The brook stopped talking, and the wind held its breath. The rough meadow grass stiffened. The Druid Oak stretched huge arms toward her, then tore itself out of the ground and hobbled toward her on its twisted roots. The birds, shaken from their nests, chided as they came. Finn would have fled the tree, but Amara pushed him into the thick of its brush. He tried to lunge away, but could not break loose; he was tangled in a vine. Amara laughed and wound another coil of vine about him, binding him fast.

"Do not struggle, foolish one," said Amara. "Let him take you into his oaken embrace. Do you not know him? He is the Sacred Oak, broken shadow of the eldest god, which has taken root in this field, and drinks its living waters, and grows huge and lusty, putting out blossoms, dropping acorns. He is a god, a rough wooden shade-giving god. He is the oak of your clan, Finn, vined by mistletoe, that magic loop. Yield . . . yield. . . . It is a father's embrace. He is of your father too, this oak; his long taproot drinks of dead kings."

Finn stopped struggling. In the music of her voice, he gave himself to the idea of oak. A green drowse fell upon him, and he slept.

When he awoke he was sitting in the shade of the Druid Oak, which had rooted itself again. Dusk had fallen, and a cold wind blew. Amara spoke to him:

"You have taken a step toward understanding. Now do this. Strip yourself naked despite the cold, or rather because of the cold, so that you will be frozen away from your own self, so that your blood will slow, and a silence come upon you, and a stillness upon your fancy, and you will invent nothing, and claim nothing, but give yourself to perfect attention. Then, after three days, we will come together, and I shall hear what you have learned."

And so it was done. After three days Finn sank into the ground past the roots of grass and flowers and the gnarled clutch of the oak to a warm place where waters are born out of underground steam. There he thawed, and clawed his way up again into light, disturbing moles.

Amara was waiting for him under the oak tree. "Did you dwell in that darkness?" she said.

"Yes."

"In the silence?"

"I did."

"Were you cold?"

"I was."

"Did the darkness and the silence and the cold help you to perfect attention?"

"They did."

"Did light come to you in the darkness?"

"The only light came from a kind of dream which happened outside my head, not inside. A bright picture floated before me in the darkness. I saw low burned hills and a flash of sea. And things tearing at the earth, pecking metal lizards all over, eating every inch of space, swarming on the beaches, filling the air with a brown oily smell—coming out of the earth to eat the living green. I felt my heart being devoured, Amara, as I watched the metal lizards eating the trees, and soiling the sand, and drinking the margins of the sea. What were they? What did I see?"

"Mineral devils."

"And what are they?"

"They belong to the kingdom of Vilemurk. As Frost Demon and Lord of Misrule he is King of the Mineral Devils. But you saw more in your vision. What else did you see?"

"It was too horrible. I cannot bear to remember."

"You are my warrior. You must look horror in the face, and not flinch. Tell me what you saw."

"The mineral devils making a mineral masterpiece. A great egg which breaks into mineral fire when it is laid by mineral birds. The birds were in the air, dropping their eggs of fire, smashing cities, igniting the dust, fusing bones and beams, roasting the cattle in the fields and the fish in the lake." His face was wet with tears. "What was it, Amara, what did I see?"

"You saw man himself as mineral devil. In your vision of time to come, he has turned away from the living gods and worships himself as mineral devil. Vilemurk triumphs. Lyr is dead, and I am dead. Man has turned his trees to spikes, his grass to barbs, and his path is stone."

"Will this come to pass? Must it be?"

"There is no 'must' in human affairs, oh, boy-who-would-be-a-man. That is a Vilemurk idea. The mineral devils want man to believe that his future can be read in the cold and mathematical stars. And so man loses hope, loses joy, and abandons himself to the devil-gods of industry, artifice, order. He trades his warm living body for a cold idea. Sells himself to the smith demons, chains himself to a stone, and stokes the forge-fires until he drops from exhaustion or is flogged to death. You know. You were a slave in the smithy."

"I did not sell myself. I was captured. And I escaped. Killed my captors and escaped—with a marvelous sword."

"Yes, you escaped. And made your way here to be my warrior. But you will not use that sword when you fight Goll McMorna."

"Not use my blue sword? Why not?"

"It is made of metal, and metal belongs to Vilemurk."

"The sword belongs to me."

"Its metal belongs to Vilemurk and will not serve you. Goll McMorna is Vilemurk's man. Right now he is in the smithy, being armed by the mineral devils. They are dressing him in metal. When he faces you he will wear brass armor and carry an iron sword."

"How will I be armed?"

"With a hawthorne stick and bag of seed. You will wear no armor, but a light woolen tunic, dyed green. Nor iron hat, but a crown of leaves. You will wield a hawthorne club. At your belt will hang a bag of seed."

"And Goll will be wearing—what again?"

"Breastplate and greaves of bright brass. He will carry a spear for throwing, and a huge two-handed sword for closework—and a battle-axe slung."

"A stick against a sword?" said Finn. "Goll is a fearsome warrior in his own right, you know, even without this inequality of arms. What chance will I have?"

"The chance I give you. Which means the chance you give yourself."

"I don't understand."

"Your weapons will do for you only what you do for them. You must make them extensions of yourself. Infuse them with your own virtue. They will respond to your courage; smite with your strength, take their edge from your fineness."

"A stick against a sword . . . wood against iron. . . ."

"Wood is alive. Iron is wood, long dead. The devils are dead gods."

"Help me to understand."

"You have seen a horrible vision of man as mineral devil, consuming the earth with mineral fire. But that vision will begin to come true only on the day when the weapons that man wields are stronger than man himself. On that day he begins to lose both strength and honor, and gives himself to the mineral devils. Do you understand?"

"I'm trying to."

"You have come to me, Amara, Goddess of Growing Things. You are son of the oak, harvest prince, my green hero. You cannot bear metal. You must use the living tools I give you."

"Shall I cut my stick from that hawthorne tree?"

"I'll break it off. No blade must touch it."

"And the bag of seed?"

"I'll teach you its use."

Amara taught Finn how to use the seeds. They were acorns of the Druid Oak. Now the roots of an oak tree go very deep. They sink themselves into the soil as far as they can, and grapple the earth hungrily. The bigger the tree, the longer the roots. And this Druid Oak, as we know, was the biggest tree in all Eire, and perhaps in all the world.

"Keep the acorns in your pouch," Amara said. "And keep the pouch at your belt. The seeds will hunger to sink themselves into the earth and put out roots, so that you will be given an enormous family pull toward the earth. Each time you touch the earth you will feel new strength coursing through your body, the incredible stubborn sappy strength of living things—the green strength, the magical plant strength which can push a tiny flower through a floor of stone, the flower we call saxifrage. So imagine what power it gives to the oak and the seeds of the oak. And that power, Finn, will flow through you when you touch the earth. With sword and battle-axe, Goll will try to beat down your guard, and beat you to earth. But, if he does, you will drink of its strength and arise renewed."

"And the seeds stay always in the pouch?" said Finn. "And the pouch at my belt?"

"Only if you know that you face death the next instant may you take a seed from the pouch. Then take only one, and cast it upon the earth. But remember—only if you face death. If you do it before that time you will have scattered your strength, and must fall under the blows of your enemy."

"I shall remember," said Finn.

"Go now. I shall watch over you. I—Amara, Lady of the Grove,

Bride of the Oak, Queen of the Harvest, Goddess of Growing Things. Take of my strength. Drink of my bounty. Strike a blow for the quick, the living, the warm-blooded. Blessings of the seed be upon you, of the root and the blossom. Murmurous blessings of the leaves. Be of good cheer, have no fear, strike with joy. The grace of all natural strokes be with you—from tiger-paw to leaf-fall. Bless you, Finn, bless you. Your victory is ours."

She knelt and took him into her meadow-sweet embrace, kissed him upon the lips, and then disappeared, leaving him reeling with happiness and unafraid.

All of Eire had to come to see the battle, it seemed. Upon the great plain of Meath before the walls of Tara were assembled the bravest and fairest in all the land. The fog-wall had blown away. A slant sun fell; the air was blue and smoky. Tents and pavilions flashed upon the plain, striped blue and crimson. Struck into the ground stood a forest of pennants—the colors of the warrior chiefs, colors of the fighting clans. The tents of the Fianna were green and gold; they sat in one cluster. These men were the picked warriors in all Ireland; it was for their chieftainship that Finn had challenged Goll. The High King sat on the royal stone—three slabs of rock forming a natural throne—on a hill overlooking the plain. The king sat there, his gold crown on his head, gold staff in his hand. His Royal Guard surrounded him. Standing there too, leaning on their spears, were the twelve brothers of Goll McMorna, underchiefs of the Fianna. The ladies of the court stood with their men. They wore beautiful gowns of silk and wreaths of flowers in their hair. They were tall and free-limbed and easy-laughing. They often accompanied their men into battle, and were sometimes more feared than the men themselves.

There were others there too—a dreadful legion whom no one saw. They had the power of keeping themselves invisible to mortal eye until they chose to appear. These were Vilemurk's cohorts, summoned there to help Goll, if needed. There were the mist-crones, and the frost demons, the Master of Winds, and Vilemurk himself, of course. He was too important for complete invisibility though; all you could see of him was the edge of his beard, like a fleecy cloud.

The king raised his staff. Trumpets cried. Goll McMorna entered the field, riding a huge black horse. Lances of sunlight shivered on his breastplate of brass and his brass greaves. On his head was an iron hat topped by a peacock feather. He carried a long spear for throwing, a great two-handed sword for closer work, and a battle-axe slung. A mighty shout arose when he appeared. He stood in his stirrups and shook his spear. The shouting doubled and redoubled until the glade rang with the voices of the fighting men of Eire. The Fianna added its keening eagle war cry, and each clan answered with its own battle shout.

Then, Finn came onto the field. There was a great collective sighing gasp of wonder and disappointment. He didn't seem like he was coming to fight at all. Where Goll was all massive heaviness and brassy strength, Finn—clad in green, unmounted, walking through the grass—seemed to have the lightness of the meadow grass itself, which he barely disturbed as he walked. Light-footed he came. He wore no armor, only his light woolen tunic, dyed green. On his head was a crown of oak leaves. All he carried in the way of arms was a hawthorne stick and a wicker shield. At his belt was a leather bag.

The king raised his staff again. The trumpets sounded a challenge. Finn stood on the grass, facing Goll, and called:

"I, Finn McCool, son of Cuhal, grandson of the Oak, wearer of Amara's green, accuse you, Goll, son of Morna, of my father's murder and wrongful claim to the chieftainship of the Fianna. I challenge you to mortal combat."

Goll sat on his horse like a brass statue. His voice rang like brass as he answered:

"I, Goll McMorna, scourge of the clan Cuhal, chief of the Fianna, wearing tomorrow's bright metal, give the lie to your accusations. I accuse you of conduct unbecoming a member of the Fianna. I accuse you of salmon-poaching, witch-baiting, and the foul magic of weather-tampering. I accept your challenge, and shall prove your guilt upon your body."

The king raised his staff again; the trumpets sounded a third time. The fight began.

Goll set his lance, crouched in his saddle, and spurred his horse into a thundering gallop. Finn stood there, waiting. The crowd gasped, seeing the slender youth hold his ground before the huge horse hurtling toward him. At the very last second Finn seemed to sway without moving his feet. Goll's lance whistled past his shoulder; the great horse rushed past, just grazing his tunic, and hurtled past to the other side of the field before Goll could rein him up, and turn him.

Finn stood there waiting, a smile on his face. He still had not moved his feet. Goll charged again. Again it happened. Finn simply swayed like a river reed touched by a breeze. Again the stallion's shoulder grazed his tunic as he stormed past. And Finn stood there, unhurt, still smiling.

Now Goll changed his tactics. He made the horse walk slowly, as a cat stalking a bird, over the field toward Finn. Goll poised himself in the saddle, sword held high. Finn left his place then, and circled very slowly, crouching slightly, holding his wicker shield in one hand and hawthorne stick in the other. Goll walked his horse in tightening circles around Finn until he towered over the boy—then raised his sword, and brought it crashing down. The crowd shouted at this terrific blow, expecting to see the heavy blade split Finn vertically, like a cook slicing a celery stalk. Finn held up his wicker shield slantwise so that the sword fell upon it, not full, but glancingly, and was deflected. The blow was so powerful that Goll almost fell from his saddle, but he recovered quickly, raised his sword again, and struck another blow, which, this time, Finn deflected with a whisk of his stick. It was a blow so swift it was almost invisible, slashing Goll across the wrist at the moment of downstroke, so that the huge blade was again deflected, but this time with terrible effect.

The edge of the blade hit Goll's horse full upon the chest. The black stallion whinnied with agony, and threw himself backward, flinging Goll clear, then rolling over the grass in his death throes. But the man was such a superb warrior he did not allow this fall to unbalance him, but twisted in the air, and landed crouching on his feet. Goll rushed toward Finn, slashing with his sword. Finn circled slowly, weaving shield and stick, deflecting the heavy blows. But Goll was enraged by the death of his horse. He was swept by battle fury, fired with a savage strength such as he had never known. He battered at Finn with his heavy sword until, finally, the blade sheared through the wicker shield—which turned it enough so that the flat of the blade fell upon Finn's shoulder. But it was a paralyzing blow. Finn felt his arm and shoulder go numb. Before he could recover, Goll had cut at him with a vicious back-handed stroke, slashing his right arm, and he could barely hold the hawthorne stick.

He leaped aside to avoid a third blow, but was so weakened by loss of blood he fell to earth. Finn immediately felt a giant sappy strength flowing through him—stanching the blood, filling him with an ecstasy of vigor. An amazed Goll saw the youth, beaten to earth a second before, spring up and face him again, smiling.

Now Finn moved so lightly that to try to strike him was like attacking a butterfly with a club. He floated away from Goll's blows, then slid in again jabbing with his pointed stick, stinging like a hornet. Again and again he touched Goll on the parts of his body not covered by brass—his arms, his legs above the greaves, his face beneath the helmet.

The crowd, wondering, saw the mighty Goll stop and stand, bewildered, like a man attacked in the glade by a swarm of hornets. They saw him wipe the blood from his face and paw with his sword. But Finn was all about him, slashing, dancing in and out so fast the eye could not follow, and Goll could not touch him with his blade.

Now Vilemurk took a hand. He whistled up a hailstorm—a small one—which fell on the field from a cloudless sky, and spat ice in Finn's path as he stalked toward the confused Goll. And Finn, stepping across the field, ready for a final attack, full of confidence and cold joy, suddenly felt his feet slipping . . . slipping . . . slipping. He shuffled desperately, trying to keep his balance—for Goll had recovered and was coming toward him.

Then, he lost sight of Goll completely. He saw nothing. He was blinded by a moist grayness that pressed upon him, snuffing the sun, and blotting his sight. The crowd lost sight of him, and could not understand. Where he stood was a slender column of fog. What had happened was that a mist-crone, obeying Vilemurk's command, had flown down invisibly to join the hailstorm, and cast her fog upon Finn, fitting it closely as a garment.

Goll, standing on the sunny field, saw the misty shape of his foe, stumbling and groping, and was able to approach without any danger to himself. He walked up to the column of mist, and began to slash it with his sword, slashing again and again, leaving the mist in tatters.

The men of the Fianna raised their eagle cry as they saw Finn stagger out of the fog, bleeding from a hundred wounds. They saw him sway, bleeding, and sink to earth. But Vilemurk understood now that Finn was renewing himself every time he touched the earth, and he would not let that happen again. He whistled a third time. The Master of Winds shook a small tornado out of his cloak—a black funneling spout of wind. It whirled down on Finn, seized him, whirled him on the grass, bleeding as he was, then lifted him into the air and kept him aloft so that he could not touch the earth.

Finn hung in the air, bleeding, almost dead. Goll had thrown off his helmet. He walked slowly to where Finn floated, shoulder-high, drawing his dagger as he went. Goll's hair was red as blood. His face was greenish-white, cheese-colored, dewed with sweat, twitching with delight. He wound his left hand into Finn's black hair, and drew back his head, stretching his neck. Then he raised his knife.

Finn's thoughts were dim as his life bled away. He felt the hand of his enemy on his head, but in his dimness the heavy hand felt like a caress. A thought floated free:

"Time to cast the seed, for, surely, I'll never be any closer to death than this."

His fingers twitched at his belt, but he had lost too much strength. He could not untie the leather pouch and cast the seed. He saw Goll's knife glittering above his head.

Then, in the hills, Amara laughed.

Goll was taking his time, raising the knife high, admiring how it flashed in the sun, knowing the crowd was hypnotized by the flashing blade too, and that they were watching him, Goll, standing triumphant over his helpless foe. As the knife glittered, Amara laughed. Finn with his last failing sense heard her laugh. And Goll heard Amara laugh. He stood there, arm high, transfixed by the wild music of her laughter. All the vast crowd heard that laughter.

No one knew what it was; no one had heard anything like it. There was something of the hawk's cry in her laughter, and of lark-thronging dawns. Of the tumbling of waters. Of mare trumpeting, answering stallion on the hill. In her laughter was gaudy summer and the million-voiced murmur of grass . . . and the hush of a pumpkin moon.

The dimming spark of Finn's life flickered in the gust of that laughter, and flared briefly. His fingers twitched again at the mouth of the pouch, and worked it open. He plucked an acorn from the bag and let it drop upon the earth—just as Goll recovered from his hesitation and slashed downward at Finn's throat.

The seed was quicker. An oak sapling sprouted with magic speed, striking Goll's arm, knocking the dagger aside. A hedge of saplings sprang up between Finn and Goll, shutting Goll off from his prey, forcing them farther and farther apart—one sapling then another springing from the ground, locking their branches, twining their twigs, making a brambly hedge for Goll—a leafy cell. He struggled and plunged but could not free himself. Vines caught his legs and his arms. He was a prisoner of growth.

Vilemurk saw what was happening. He gestured to the Master of Winds who immediately flung a sharp-edged gale to scythe down the hedge. But the downdraft of the gale hit Finn, and pressed him to earth. As soon as he touched earth his wounds closed; his mind cleared. A sappy green strength coursed through him, and he sprang to his feet, bright as morning.

The gale scythed down the saplings. The hedge was falling. Goll was struggling free. Finn picked up his hawthorne stick and let himself be taken by the gale. He went flying across the field like a leaf—going with enormous speed, holding the pointed stick. And when he hit Goll he had all the force of the gale behind him—that force which has been known to drive a splinter of wood through a stone wall. The hawthorne stick went through the brass breastplate like a needle through cloth and came out the other side. Goll fell heavily, gaffed like a trout.

Finn stood over him, hair ruffled by the wind, eyes glowing. He raised his hawthorne stick on high, and lifted his voice in the great victory cry of the Fianna. The Fianna called back, shrieking like eagles. He was their chief now.

Finn looked down at Goll. He was not yet dead. He was saying something. Finn knelt to listen.

"Water," Goll whispered. "Bring water. . . ."

Now it will be remembered that when Finn cooked the Loutish Trout he had scorched his hand, and that scorch was magical. His burned thumb gave him the gift of prophecy when he bit it. And the scorched palm had the power of saving life. If he brought water in his cupped hands, and gave it to a dying man to drink—that man would be given life.

"Water . . . ," moaned Goll. "Please. . . ."

Finn hesitated, then crossed the field to where a spring of pure water gushed from the earth. He took the water in his cupped palms, and crossed back toward Goll. His hands opened as he walked. The water spilled. He came to Goll and looked down at him. The man was still alive, and his whisper came again, even more faintly.

"Water . . . water. . . ."

Finn kept looking at him. No one in the crowd had left. They were all watching what was happening without understanding. They saw the green figure of Finn cross the sunny grass to where the spring flashed. Saw him kneel and take water in his hands and bring it back toward Goll. Then, as he came, they saw his hands fall to his side; he wiped his wet palms on his tunic. He came and looked down at Goll. Now the man was dead.

Finn lifted his face toward the sky. He was not smiling. His face was not that of a boy, but of a man—who kills.

But Finn was doubly wrong. Wrong to refuse aid to a dying

man, foe or not. Wrong in leaving a great gift unused. At the very moment of his victory, when life should have been blossoming most hotly for him, Finn had twice said No to life . . . and, at that moment was no better than the man of iron he had defeated.

He realized his mistake later, and went on to become Ireland's greatest hero. Nevertheless, he was to pay dearly for his treatment of Goll McMorna. But that is part of another story.